THE ENCHANTER'S NEW KIDS

THE ELLWOOD CHRONICLES V

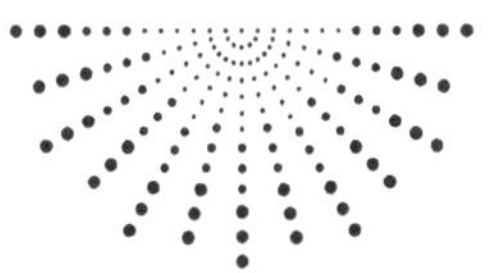

MICHELE NOTARO

Edited by: TRIBE Editing
Proofreading by: Jill Wexler

The amazing book cover was done by:
Soxsational Cover Art

This is a gay romance that contains adult language, adult situations, and sexually explicit material between two men. It is intended for ADULTS ONLY.

AUTHOR'S NOTE

Thank you for picking up *The Enchanter's New Kids*. If you haven't read the rest of *The Ellwood Chronicles* yet, I highly recommend starting with *The Enchanter's Flame* so you can easily follow the story and characters in this book.

If you've read *The Ellwood Chronicles*, you know that the prophecy has been fulfilled and the main storyline has been completed. This story is simply for the fun of being back with Seb and Ailin, getting to see them comfortable and happy in their relationship—the world finally at peace—and watch them adopt a few more kids. It's shorter than the other books, but still filled with their love, and of course, their bickering.

This book was written as something fun and extra, and is quite literally, about their new kids. So if you enjoy reading about kid antics and the craziness that comes with being a parent, this one's for you. As crazy as parenting is, can you imagine if your kids had magic on top of it? Thank goodness for small miracles (my boys can be wild enough without it).

I hope you enjoy this fun and heartfelt story about family and the love Ailin and Seb share with each other and the rest of the Ellwood coven.

With Love,
Michele

PROLOGUE

AILIN

I heard the screaming the second I got out of the car. At first I panicked, but then I took a deep breath and realized that Sebastian would've told me through our telepathic bond that something was wrong, so everything must be fine. Well, not *fine*, since there was screaming, but at the very least, no one was dying.

Get your ass in here! Seb yelled in my head, making me jump and slam the car door shut before rushing up the porch.

The screaming only intensified as I opened the front door, and I realized why Seb had been actively blocking me all day. He and I could access one another's minds, in a sense, and we were always aware of each other's emotions and whereabouts. But as soon as I'd walked into the meeting with the head official of our government, Seb had told me everything was fine and immediately blocked me. I trusted him implicitly so I didn't bother him about it, figuring we'd talk when I got home.

Now I was grateful he'd kept the distraction from me.

Walking deeper into the house, I could hear the baby screaming at the top of his lungs, louder than any cry we'd heard yet. And along with his screaming cries was the sound of a yelling four-year-old as she ran with a blanket strapped around her neck like a cape and her feet sounding like a herd of elephants stomping through the whole house. I stopped in my tracks as I rounded the corner and found an eleven-year-old with her feet up on the couch, a sketchpad in her lap, and earbuds in her ears with Sebastian standing in front of her bouncing the baby and trying to get the pre-teen's attention.

When Seb turned to me, he looked absolutely exhausted—even more so than when he'd had most of his soul eaten by a damn elder ogre—his hair was sticking up in every direction, he had spit-up on his shoulder and a billion stains on his shirt that I wasn't sure I wanted to know about, and looked just about in tears himself.

Relief flowed through our link as his shoulders sagged at the sight of me, and he marched right over, thrust the baby in my arms, and said, "Never leave me alone with them again."

I put the baby over my shoulder, patting his back to see if he needed to burp.

Seb backed away quickly with his hands out like he was going to fend me off if I tried to pass the baby back. "He pooped." He walked over to the changing table and opened up a new package of diapers, saying over his shoulder to the eleven-year-old, "Was it really that difficult to help open these?" Then he ran past me, yelling over the screaming, "Good luck with that. I'm taking a shower… where I can cry in peace." The last part was said to himself, but I'd caught it through our link. He grimaced in my direction, then disappeared up the stairs.

The four-year-old ran right up to me and punched me in the thigh, making me yell out. "Ow! Why would you do that?" What the hell?

"I'm a superhero," she said before screaming at the top of her lungs and running away again.

I called after her, "You don't hit people!"

"But you're a bad guy! Good guys hit the bad guys!"

When did she become so violent? Before I could yell at her, the eleven-year-old pulled an earbud out, pointed at me, and said, "You've got baby puke dripping off your shoulder, and I'm pretty sure there's poop coming out the back of his pants."

Looking down, I wrinkled my nose as I examined the poop that was now on my hands. "Aw shit."

"You said a bad word!" was yelled a moment before I got another punch to my thigh.

"Ow! Don't hit me! You're going on time out!"

"Not if you can't catch me!"

My eyes widened at the bratty response, and I watched the four-year-old superhero run away, but the baby burped and I felt more puke being added to my shoulder, so I didn't run after her. "Shit. Can you please go grab your sister?"

The eleven-year-old shrugged, acted as if I hadn't asked for her help, and stuffed her earbud back in.

"Not cool," I muttered as I rushed over to the changing table. *Seb, when are you coming back down?*

Never.

Sebastian. Come on.

I swear to god, Ailin. I've had them all day, you can deal with them for twenty minutes while I take a shower and get the baby's poop out of my hair!

I blinked at that, then stared down at the baby squirming on the changing table. *How did you get poop in your hair?*

You don't want to know.

I pulled the clothes off the baby, and the second I opened his diaper, something wet hit me in the face. It only took me a second to realize it was pee. Home for one minute and I was already covered in horrors.

With a sigh, I tried to block out all the screaming as I scrubbed the little guy clean. *Sebastian?* I thought to my viramore—my soulmate.

What?

I love you.

I love you, too.

You know you're gorgeous, right? And amazing.

There was a pause before he said through our link, *Being nice to me isn't going to get me to come back down there any faster.*

I snorted. *Worth a try.*

Don't worry, only two hours until bedtime.

MICHELE NOTARO

Holy fuck.
Tell me about it.

CHAPTER ONE

SEBASTIAN

TWO MONTHS EARLIER

"We don't have to go in," my viramore—my soulmate—said as he reached for my hand and squeezed it before placing a kiss to my palm. "I can run the box up, and we can go right home."

I glanced at him, my Ailin. He was in the driver's seat, his bright green eyes full of concern, his long black hair braided back on one side while the rest hung loose around his shoulder. We'd been together for around six years now, and still I sometimes couldn't believe my luck. He still dressed in all black, reminding me of the goth kid I thought he was the first time we'd met, only now I saw the softer sides of him, too. Outside of our home, he was tough, annoyed with just about everyone that dared to speak to him, and typically an overall asshole, but at home he was… well, still an asshole, but now I knew how much he cared about his family, about me, about everyone, really.

"I am not an asshole," he muttered, overhearing my thoughts. Since he was my viramore, we could speak telepathically, and sometimes strong thoughts ended up seeping through our connection.

"Yes, you are," I said and leaned over to kiss his shoulder. "But you're my asshole." As soon as those words were out of my mouth, my eyes widened, and Ailin laughed, so I put my hand over his mouth. "Don't say it."

"But I want to," he mumbled around my hand, then swiped his tongue over my palm.

"Ew. Come on, you child."

He kissed my palm. "I thought I was your asshole?" He grinned.

I pushed his shoulder, shaking my head. "What I meant was that you are a giant ass, but you have the biggest heart of anyone I know."

"Don't be sappy with me."

"It's the truth."

"Trying to get into my pants, detective?"

"As if I have to try."

Chuckling, he leaned across the console to kiss my neck over the top of my vitmea mark—a spell he'd cast to bind us together that left marks like tattoos on our necks—making me shiver. To pay him back, I lightly brushed my fingers over his vitmea mark. He smirked and ran his hand through my hair, muttering words in another language under his breath. I had no idea what the hell he was saying. It could've been poetry or he could've been cussing me out—I'd give it fifty-fifty odds, it seriously could go either way, and the bastard spoke a billion languages, so I could never keep up.

I cut him off. "Ailin?"

"Sebastian."

I sighed and said, "No starting shit in the car. Look where we are." I gestured to the huge, looming building in front of us.

He huffed and rolled his eyes, then kissed the back of my hand and held it tight in his. "What do you want to do, Seb?"

"You really want me to meet these girls?"

"Yes, baby."

"Then we'll go in."

His green eyes flicked back and forth, taking me in and probably seeing more than I was comfortable with before he nodded and said, "We can sit in the car for a bit longer."

"You're being really understanding even though I know you're dying to go inside."

He shrugged.

"Thank you."

"See, I'm not always an asshole."

I grinned at that. "Just most of the time."

"Well, people are usually idiots, so…"

I snorted and leaned back in my seat to stare at the stupid building again. It wasn't that I didn't want to go and meet these girls Ailin had been talking about for the past two weeks, it was that I didn't want to get hit with the memories that came with that building.

The Eastbrook Youth Academy was the orphanage I'd been dropped off at when I was a baby, so I grew up here. Only back when I was a kid, this place was basically a military school that cared about one thing: making good soldiers. There was no time for fun and games when they were busy making us their puppets, and there certainly was no room for love within those walls.

Growing up, I'd thought I was human because there was a binding spell on me hiding my enchanter nature, and even though I hadn't known magic was real back then, some of it had still trickled in. Enough to give me nightmares nearly every night, nightmares that felt so real, I thought monsters were attacking me. And so, the Head Lady would lock me in solitary confinement when the nightmares were bad —as if I'd been able to control what I was dreaming about. I'd been hit, cut, starved, and all kinds of other terrible things growing up. This place still gave me nightmares as an adult.

Luckily, the world was a better place now. The magical community had revealed itself about five years ago during the Berserker War. Since we'd won the war, humans and magical creatures alike had been working together to find peace. And we had. There was still devastation and heartbreak that needed fixing after the war—there would be for a long time—but we were trying, and we were doing it together.

Many, many lives had been lost, so there were a lot of children that no longer had homes and families. In response, the new government

—The Brinnswick Union—had taken over Eastbrook Youth Academy, and now the misplaced children were treated with kindness and love.

But that didn't exactly erase my memories of the place.

Ailin whispered, "Do you want me to take you home?"

Turning to him, I examined his features again. He was damn gorgeous on the outside, but even more so on the inside. He had so much love to give, and… he'd been wanting to adopt more kids—yes, *more*. Ailin raised about a million kids when all the adults in his coven were killed and he took over as coven leader at sixteen. But now all the kids were grown and out of the house, and Ailin wanted more. Or specifically, he wanted to raise a handful of kids *with me*. It was something he'd been dreaming about for years, and maybe a little of those dreams had rubbed off on me because I *maybe* wanted that as well. Okay, I *did* want it, but I didn't want to admit it to him.

I offered him a smile and whispered, "I'm ready. Let's go in."

"You sure?"

"Yeah, sweetheart. Introduce me to your girls."

The smile that overtook his face was beautiful and had me grinning back at him as we climbed out of the car. Taking a deep breath, I let him lead me up the path and through the doors. A gasp fell from my lips as I came to a sudden stop.

The foyer and staircase were covered with bright colors, a wall with hundreds of children's artwork hanging on it, and the stairs were even painted. Over the walkway that led to the large cafeteria—or what used to be the mess hall—was a sign that read *Love is Stronger*.

When the sounds of children's laughter reached my ears coming from a room I used to hate, my eyes pricked with tears that I blinked away. Turning to Ailin, I whispered, "It really is different here, isn't it?"

A surge of sadness came through our bond followed by the vast love he felt for me, and he whispered, "Yeah, baby, it is." He stepped in front of me, placing his hand on the side of my neck. "Are you okay? We can turn around if you need to."

I shook my head. "I'm okay. I want to see the rest."

He smiled gently. "Alright, but tell me if you need to leave."

"I will."

We weren't usually the hand-holding type when we were out, but when Ailin grabbed my hand and laced our fingers together, I clung to him.

A woman I didn't know came rushing out of the room where giggles were following her, and when she saw my viramore, she smiled widely, saying, "Ailin, it's so good to see you, honey."

"Hi, Mrs. Hunley. This is my viramore, Sebastian," he said. "Seb, Mrs. Hunley." She held out her hand to shake, and I stared at it for a moment before Ailin said in my head, *She's human, you can shake her hand.* I'd learned the hard way not to ever touch a magical creature's hand in greeting—it had taken years to break that habit.

With a grin, I shook and said, "It's nice to meet you. I've heard wonderful things about you and everything you've done here."

She smiled wider. "That's great to hear. Ailin talks about you all the time."

He grumbled beside me as I said, "Don't believe anything he says."

She laughed and Ailin squeezed my fingers, but I knew he was amused.

Mrs. Hunley asked us, "I assume you're here to see Leilani and Niya?"

Ailin nodded. "Yes. And I was hoping to show Seb around. I wanted him to see how great this place is now."

She nodded, and I huffed out a breath before admitting, "I grew up here, but it wasn't"—I waved my free hand around—"like this at all."

A flash of sympathy rushed over her features. "I'm sorry to hear that, Sebastian. I hope you'll find the things we're doing here positive."

I laughed humorlessly. "Trust me, just being this far inside, I can tell it is."

Another look of sympathy from her made me wish I hadn't said anything, and Ailin picked up on my discomfort and said, "How about we head back? I assume the girls are in the art room?"

She nodded. "Most likely. I've been in there"—she pointed behind her—"reading a book to some of the younger ones. I'm sure Ms.

Summers knows where they are if they're not in there painting with her. You okay to walk around alone?"

Ailin nodded. "Yes. Do you have a list for me today?"

She grinned and pulled a piece of paper from her pocket. "Only a couple of things. Thank you, Sage. We all really appreciate your help."

"No problem. I'll take care of this after I take Seb to meet the girls."

She nodded. "Let me know when you leave, please."

"I will."

She shot me a smile before going back into the room, and her voice drifted back to us. "Now, where were we? On a safari?"

A bunch of kids yelled, "No!" with laughter, and one voice said, "We were on a pirate ship!"

"Oh, that's right. Silly me, I forgo—" Her voice cut off as the doors closed behind her.

"Come on, baby," Ailin said, pulling me along, tucking the box he'd brought under his arm and the paper in his pocket. He managed to do that without releasing my hand, which was a good thing since I was clinging to it.

"Is that a list of things for you to fix?" I asked as we walked under the *Love is Stronger* sign.

"Yes. Since I've been coming here once a week, I told her to start writing things down that I can fix with my magic."

I nodded, then got distracted by the huge room we walked into. It was light and bright and colorful, and full of happy children that were eating on one side of the room while the other side had a game of tag going on. I had to blink at the sight. I hadn't even realized those windows were there when I was here. It used to be so dark and dreary in here. They must've had curtains or been covered in paint when I was a kid. The sunlight made it feel like a different place entirely.

"The art room is on the other side of the hall, come on." Ailin pulled me through the center of the hall, and a few of the kids waved to him.

I shouldn't have been surprised. Ailin loved kids, he always had, and I knew he wished he could take home each and every one of them. Seeing how many kids were waving and how happy Ailin seemed made me feel a little bad for calling him an asshole before we came inside.

Ailin rolled his eyes at me, shaking his head. *Don't feel bad. If this room was full of adults, you bet your ass I wouldn't be acting like this.*

That is true. I grinned at him.

He knocked on a door and a voice yelled, "Come in," so he opened it, dragging me inside an art studio that was covered in artwork and lots and lots of paint drips all over the place. It kinda looked like someone flicked paint around on purpose.

"Ms. Summers, this is my viramore, Sebastian," Ailin said to the art teacher, who I could tell was a werewolf.

"Nice to meet ya," she said to me, shooting me a grin and *not* trying to shake my hand.

"You too."

She nodded toward the back of the room. "The girls are over there."

"Thanks." Ailin pulled me to the back of the room where two very adorable little girls were.

Since Ailin had been talking about them for weeks, I knew that Leilani was eleven years old, and her younger sister Niya was only four. I also knew that they were half-human, half-nymph. They both had bright blue eyes that stood out against their dark skin and brown hair, although Leilani's was loosely curled while Niya's was super curly and cute.

Niya glanced up from her painting as we walked over, and as soon as her eyes landed on Ailin, her whole face lit up. She threw her paintbrush down and came running. Ailin released my hand to squat down and catch the little girl as she launched into his arms, and as soon as I saw Ailin hug her, as soon as I felt how much he already loved this little one, I knew without a shadow of a doubt that she was meant to be our daughter.

Ailin's gaze snapped to mine over Niya's head, his eyes wide and questioning. He'd heard my thoughts.

I nodded to him, and said through our link, *Yeah, sweetheart. She's ours.*

He closed his eyes and hugged the little girl tighter, kissing the side of her head. They stayed that way for a long time, and seeing it, seeing and feeling his love and joy, it made me wish I would've come here with him sooner.

You're here now.

I know, but we could've had her home with—

It doesn't matter. Come meet her. He leaned back and quietly said to the little girl, "I want you to meet someone." He gestured to me. "This is Sebastian. He's my viramore, do you know what that is?"

She nodded. "Leilani said it's a soulmate."

We both smiled, and I said, "That's right. I'm Ailin's soulmate. He's told me so much about you, it's nice to finally meet you." I squatted down beside them so I was on their level.

She eyed me for a few long moments before smiling. "Do you like to paint?"

"I do, but I'm not very good at it."

"I can teach you!" She hopped off Ailin and grabbed my hand, pulling me over to her easel.

"She's never going to let you go now," he said with a laugh before he walked over to the eleven-year-old. He fist-bumped her. "Hey, Leilani. How have you been this week?"

The girl shrugged and continued drawing in her sketchbook.

"You looked like you were running low on pencils, so I brought you some new ones." Ailin put the box he'd been carrying on the table and Leilani eyed it.

"You did?"

"Yep." He nudged the box over, and when she took it, he grinned, then pulled a small watercolor paint set out of his back pocket—I hadn't even known he'd had it there—and tossed it to me. "For Niya."

I held the little paints out to her. "This is from Ailin."

"And Seb," Ailin added without glancing up from whatever Leilani was showing him in her sketchbook.

Niya took the paints from me with a smile, yelling, "Thank you!" before she set it on the table. She handed me a paintbrush that she'd already had out and said, "You can paint the grass. I'mma make a butterfly."

"Are you sure? I don't want to mess up your painting."

"You won't, silly. It'll be fun."

"Okay." I dipped the brush into the green and started painting at the bottom of her paper while she made a huge blue blob that I guessed was her butterfly. "That's really pretty. You're a good artist."

"Thank you. Ms. Summers teaches me a lot."

"Does your sister like to paint?"

She shrugged. "She likes her pencils more. But... but she paints wif me sometimes."

"What else do you like to do?"

"I like climbing trees, but Mrs. Hunley always yells at me to get down." She leaned in like she was telling me a secret. "But I do it anway."

With a chuckle, I kept painting.

A few minutes in, Ailin walked over with the eleven-year-old, and said, "Seb, this is Leilani."

I smiled at her. "Hi, Leilani. It's nice to meet you." She waved a tiny bit, obviously being shy, and I knew that feeling, so I nodded at her sketchpad in her arms. "Ailin tells me you're a really great artist."

She glanced at Ailin, then back at me. "He does?"

"Yes. He told me you drew a really gorgeous satyr picture the other day, and onc of your sister sleeping that he thought was really good."

Her eyes widened before she glanced at Ailin, asking, "You said that?"

"Yeah, sweetie, I did. I told you that you're really good." He offered a gentle smile. "Do you want to show Seb?"

She glanced between us before her gaze landed on me. "You would want to see?"

"Of course."

She nodded and started flipping through her book before she landed on a page and passed it to me. The satyr in the picture was so detailed, I swore it could hop off the page and start dancing around right in front of me. Even the background, swirling wind carrying leaves and flowers, was incredibly detailed. I didn't know what I'd expected, but it sure as hell wasn't that. "Wow. This is amazing. I can't…" I made eye contact with her. "You sure you're only eleven?" She snorted and rolled her eyes, and for some reason that little move did it for me. She was ours, too. Not that we ever would've separated the sisters to begin with, but… she was ours.

Ailin sent me a huge smile, so I knew he'd heard that as well.

Refocusing on Leilani, I asked, "Can I see the other one?"

She shrugged. "Sure." She flipped through a few pages, then pointed at one. "I think that's the one he meant."

As I examined the drawing, another "Wow" came out of me. It looked as if she'd taken a black and white photo of her sister sleeping and just shoved it in her sketchbook. Holy shit. "This is… just wow. Phenomenal."

She rolled her eyes again, but I could see that she was pleased. "Thanks."

We stayed with the girls until it was time for them to go eat lunch. They both gave Ailin a hug, and little Niya even gave me one. Leilani waved at me as they walked out the door.

As soon as they were gone, Ailin turned to me and asked, "You really think they're ours?"

I nodded. "Yes."

He was suddenly in my arms with his face pressed to my neck and his arms around my waist. "Can we talk to Mrs. Hunley today?"

"Yeah, but you already filled out adoption paperwork, right? How soon can we take them home with us?"

"I'm not sure. It'll be at least a few days, but they know me, so that'll help."

"I'm sure being Sage helps as well." Sage was the title for the most powerful witch in the world, so…

"I hate that title, and now that the boys are back from Faela, am I even still Sage? They're more powerful than me."

"They're also something… different than you now. They're not just witches."

He sighed and waved me off. "I guess. Since the war, the adoption process has been sped up, but the regulations are actually harder. They have a lot more help than they used to, though, so it helps speed things up."

"Alright, what do we need to do?"

"We'll go find out, but let me take care of this list first, and maybe after we talk to Mrs. Hunley, we can tell the girls to make sure this is what they want."

"Sounds like a plan."

A minute later, Ailin said, "You know, it's summer vacation for kids."

"Okay…?"

"We can take off work for a while so we can get to know the girls better, spend the summer with them before they start school in the fall."

I thought about that and smiled. "That would be great… is Niya old enough for school?"

"Pre-school, yes."

I nodded, excitement buzzing between us both.

He led the way upstairs, and even though I knew this was the same building I'd grown up in, it was so full of color, life, and love that it didn't seem the same at all. Still, I stayed close to Ailin—my safe place.

Or I did until he started fixing a light in the hallway and I heard a baby crying. Following the sound, I walked around a corner and found an open door, so I peeked inside. There were a few cribs in there, but from my spot at the door, only one of them was filled. The baby cried again, and when I glanced around and realized no one was nearby, I walked into the room. I probably wasn't supposed to—I knew most people weren't allowed to walk around the facility alone, but they allowed Ailin to—and I headed for the crib.

The baby cried again, and my chest constricted. He sounded so upset it was breaking my heart. Without a thought, I found myself reaching for him and picking him up, cradling him to my chest.

"Shh, shh, shh, I've got you," I whispered. "It's okay, little guy. You're okay." I started bouncing him, and his cries turned to tiny whimpers, so I hugged him a little. "You're alright, buddy. You're okay."

"Oh," Mrs. Hunley said from the doorway, making me jump. She smiled at me. "I was all the way downstairs and couldn't get here any faster. Thanks for picking him up. He usually naps longer than that."

"I'm sorry I came in here without asking."

She waved me away. "If I didn't trust Ailin like I do, you wouldn't have been allowed on the second floor at all. It's fine." She smiled and nodded at the baby. "He likes you."

I glanced down at the bundle in my arms and saw the little baby staring up at me with huge brown eyes, just staring, no longer crying. He was the cutest thing I'd ever seen. "He's adorable. What's his name?"

"Remington." She leaned against the doorframe. "He's been here about a month now."

"Is it rude to ask why he's here? Or how?"

She shook her head. "It's fine. We found him on our doorstep, so we're not sure where he came from."

I frowned at that and stared at the baby again, then I ran my finger along his cheek and one of his tiny hands reached out to grab ahold of it. "Oh my god." I swallowed thickly. "Hey, little Remington. How are you doing today?"

You want to bring him home, too, don't you? Ailin was still working on the lights, but we were connected in every way, so of course he knew what was going on and how I was feeling.

I do. Oh my god, Ailin. You have to come see him.

And you thought I was bad. Three, Seb? You really want three new kids to take care of?

Come here, you'll see.

Be there in a sec.

I continued rocking the baby and staring into his sweet little face while Mrs. Hunley leaned against the doorjamb with a soft smile on her face. Ailin showed up a few minutes later, and as soon as he walked into the room, he froze, staring at me. As his gaze softened, he met my eyes and held them for a moment before he breathed out, "I love you."

I smiled back. "I love you, too. Come over here."

He stepped closer and pulled little Remington's blanket down so he could get a better look at his face. His big brown eyes stared up at Ailin, and I could feel my viramore melting. "He's beautiful." Ailin moved to stand behind me a little, leaning around me with his cheek resting against my arm, one hand on my lower back, the other running a fingertip over Remington's tiny hand that still held my finger. "Seb." He sounded choked up. "You sure about this?"

"Yes."

He kissed my shoulder. "Can I hold him?" I nodded and awkwardly passed the baby to him. Ailin expertly shifted him around so the baby was looking over his shoulder, and my viramore grinned at me. "Did you change him yet?" I shook my head, so he turned to Mrs. Hunley and asked, "Can I change him or do you need to?"

She waved at the changing table. "Help yourself."

Ailin chuckled and made his way over to the changing table, so I moved over to Mrs. Hunley and asked, "What do we have to do to adopt him as well as the girls?"

She lifted her eyebrows. "Are you sure you two can handle three kids?"

Was I sure? No. Not at all. Well, I wasn't sure *I* could handle them, but I knew Ailin could. And I knew we'd do everything in our power to ensure these kids were well taken care of and shown more love than anyone could imagine. But I didn't say that to her, that was something for Ailin and me to talk about, so instead, I said, "Do you know what happened when Ailin was sixteen?"

She nodded. "I've heard the stories from some of the… magic users here." She was a human, so she'd known about the magical community for only a few years—many humans were still adjusting to it. If I hadn't had a front row seat to it all, I probably would be, too.

"He took charge of fifteen other people, all younger than him from two to fifteen years old. If anyone can handle three kids, it's him."

"And what about you?"

I shrugged. "I'm willing to follow his lead on this one, and I have our whole family for support. The Ellwood family would be lucky to have all three of them."

She smiled at me and patted my arm as Ailin walked back over with the baby cooing and pulling on his hair, and I had to admit that he looked good with a baby on his hip like that. A strangled sound came out of my throat, and Ailin smirked at me, but luckily, remained quiet instead of saying some sexual innuendo that would embarrass the hell out of me and probably make her rethink giving us three kids.

I walked over, wrapped my arms around Ailin from behind, and rested my cheek against his hair as I stared at the little one. He was so adorable, and when he smiled at me, I was a goner.

"I don't want to leave him here," I whispered.

"Me either, Seb, but we need to get things set up for a baby at home, and we need to fill out about a million pages of paperwork." He turned the three of us slightly so he could make eye contact with Mrs. Hunley. "How long will the process take, do you think?"

"Since you've been volunteering here and you started the process already, plus you have a personal recommendation from Petunia Crane herself, it'll probably be about a week. These days, the process is faster in general. If we can get the paperwork processed faster than that, we will. If that's what you want?"

"Yes," I said. "As quickly as possible."

She smiled at me. "Would you two like to come to my office to start with the paperwork, then?"

"Sure," Ailin said. "Can we bring Remi with us?"

"Remi," I whispered. "I like that."

Ailin grinned over his shoulder at me.

Mrs. Hunley nodded. "Of course. We can keep him with us. He's obviously loving the attention." When she walked out of the room, I reluctantly let go of Ailin so we could follow, happy that Mrs. Hunley was so relaxed and seemed like she genuinely cared about the kids' well-beings and happiness.

"Do you want to carry him?" Ailin asked.

My eyes widened. "Uh… there's steps."

The corner of his lips twitched. "And?"

"And I can't carry a baby down the steps, Ailin."

He chuckled. "Fine. We'll work up to that."

"I'll take him when we get back down there, if you want."

Somehow, he managed to hold the baby with one arm for a few seconds so he could reach over and squeeze my hands. If I would've tried that, I'd probably drop the little guy on his head.

Ailin snorted, having overheard my thought, and said, "No you wouldn't have. But it takes practice. You'll be fine. Before you know it, you'll be running up and down the steps with him."

I shot him a terrified look that made him snort and decided to change the subject. "Mrs. Hunley? Where will Remi go after we leave? He doesn't spend all day in his crib, does he?"

"Oh no, of course not. We have a room for the babies where they get to play with others and with the staff and volunteers. Some of the older kids like to come in to spend time with the babies, too. I'll show you after we've finished."

"Thank you."

We got to the first floor, and Ailin immediately passed the baby to me. I stood there for a few seconds, trying to get my hands right, and when I finally felt comfortable, I followed them into the office.

While Mrs. Hunley went over the paperwork, I remained standing, bouncing the little guy because every time I tried to sit with him, he started crying. Ailin was amused, but he took care of the paperwork while I got to play with Remi, and whenever my viramore said I needed to sign something, I did so carefully. Holding a wiggly six-month-old with one hand was kinda scary, if I was being honest. But I got it done, and I never wanted to put the baby down again.

CHAPTER TWO

AILIN

Watching Sebastian with Remi was making me feel like my heart was growing with every damn second. He was a natural. As much as he didn't think he was good with kids, he was so patient and kind to them, and treated them all like they were the intelligent, precious beings they were. It was beautiful to watch.

You're gorgeous, I said to him.

He smiled at me, and without missing a beat of his little humming tune toward Remi, said back through our link, *Not as gorgeous as you.*

I shot him a grin before refocusing on Mrs. Hunley. I still couldn't believe we were really doing this. I knew as soon as I got Seb in here to meet Niya and Leilani, he'd want to adopt them, but it was still unbelievable. I'd wanted to raise children with Sebastian Cooper Ellwood for years, and it was finally happening.

Yes, we had all the other kids, and yes, Seb had helped me with them for the last six years, but they'd all been older, and so many of them were already grown by the time Seb came into the picture. He treated them like they were his, because they were, but I was looking forward to seeing him with younger kids—*our* younger kids. I was looking forward to seeing them call him Dad or Papa or whatever we —or they—came up with.

And I was looking forward to being able to be home with our kids more than I ever had been with my older ones. I'd had so much responsibility on my shoulders back when I'd taken over my coven. I'd been Sage, I'd been a leader in Brinnswick, and I'd had to take care of so many issues for the good of our people that I'd been out of the house more than I'd liked.

But I'd given all of that up. Yes, I was still technically an officer for the Brinnswick Union, and still Sage, but now that Brinnswick was under a good leadership I'd been able to step back. Which meant that since the war ended, I'd been there for my kids—all of them, even my grown ones—in a way I'd never been before. And when these three became a part of our family, I'd be there every step of the way.

I couldn't wait.

But unfortunately, I couldn't simply whisk them away from this place, so it would be a few days.

After we finished, we walked Remi to the baby room, and as soon as Mrs. Hunley opened the doors, I could tell that Seb was impressed with the set up. The brightly colored room was filled to the brim with educational toys, exersaucers, jumpers, and everything you could ever possibly need for a baby. It was also a lot bigger than I'd been expecting, and there were clearly areas set up for different things like floor time for younger babies, and a little fenced-in area for the crawlers, a few rocking chairs in the feeding area, a few changing tables, and a couple of cribs. And there were several volunteers inside playing with and helping care for the babies.

When I felt my chest tighten uncomfortably, I knew the strong emotions weren't my own. Seb was blown away with the change of this orphanage from the one he'd grown up in, and his emotions were all over the place because of it. He also didn't want to leave Remi here, as wonderful as this place was; he wanted Remi to come home with us.

Placing my hand on his upper back, I leaned in and whispered, "He'll be okay. We'll be back to pick him up in a few days."

He took a deep breath. "I know."

I kissed his cheek, then turned to Mrs. Hunley. "Thank you. Let me know what else you need from me to make this go as fast as possible."

"I will." She offered me a smile, then turned to Seb and said gently, "I can take him."

Seb pressed a kiss to Remi's forehead, closed his eyes, and breathed the baby in. I kept my hand on his back, letting him have his moment, and when he pulled back with glossy eyes, I kissed the baby's cheek. Mrs. Hunley pulled Remi from Seb's arms, and I reached up to my viramore's neck to rub my thumb over his vitmea mark in the hopes that it offered comfort.

I asked Mrs. Hunley, "Is it okay if Seb and I talk to the girls one last time before we leave? I want to make sure they want to be a part of our family."

She smiled widely at us. "I'm sure they would appreciate it. Since you've been vetted already, it's fine to tell them."

"Thank you. Do you need us to check in with you before we head out?"

"If you can, yes. If I'm not around, just let someone know."

With a nod, I grabbed Seb's hand, but his entire focus was on Remi.

"We'll be back," Seb whispered to Remi as Mrs. Hunley walked away toward the little feeding area in the back.

I leaned in to whisper to Seb, "We will, baby. Come on. Let's track down the girls again and make this official."

He nodded at me and let me lead him out and all the way back to the art room. It wasn't surprising that both girls were still inside. Leilani saw us first and smiled at me, asking, "You're back?"

I nodded. "We have something we want to talk to you about."

She immediately looked worried, and I didn't know how to ease that fear besides telling her, but I wanted both girls here with us.

"Niya, can you come here for a minute?" I asked.

The four-year-old seemed surprised to see us, but came over and had a seat beside her sister, both of them staring up at me with wide, nervous, bright blue eyes.

I offered a smile and sat across from them on a stool so we were in between two tables, our knees almost touching. Seb sat beside me, and after I squeezed his thigh, I refocused on the girls. Our future daughters. Even that thought had me floating. "Seb and I would like to know if you two would like to come home with us?" I cringed and added, "Not today because there's… paperwork, but would you two like to live with us?" Somehow their eyes got impossibly larger.

Sebastian cleared his throat and said, "We'd like to adopt you. Both of you."

Leilani's eyes darted between Seb and me. "Really? You want both of us?"

My brow furrowed, but Seb leaned forward, and in that sweet and soft voice of his, said, "Yes, Leilani, we want both of you. We would never want to separate you from your sister, and anyway, we really, truly want you, too."

Her eyes became glossy, and she began blinking furiously.

I rested my elbows on my knees so my face was closer to both of theirs. "We would like you to become Ellwoods, to become members of our coven, to be our… to be our daughters. Both of you."

Leilani's eyes blinked even faster, but Niya distracted me by squealing loudly and launching herself into my arms, bouncing on her toes. She was so happy and excited that a laugh bubbled out of me as I hugged her close.

After a minute, I said, "I take it that it's a yes from you, Ni?"

She nodded frantically. "Yes! Yes, yes, yes!"

I chuckled and continued hugging her, then met her sister's gaze over her shoulder. "What about you, sweetie? Would you do us the honor of becoming our daughter?"

This time when she blinked, a tear fell down her cheek, and her voice came out watery. "You really want me, too?"

"Of course we do," Seb said, his own voice sounding a little choked up.

She made eye contact with him, then nodded slowly.

Seb smiled widely at her and got up to move to the stool beside Leilani. He hesitantly put an arm around her, and after a tense moment, Leilani fell into him, accepting his offered hug. All I could do was stare at my viramore. A few years ago, he wouldn't have been comfortable enough in his own skin to offer comfort to someone he hardly knew. Sometimes he'd even had trouble offering hugs to the kids when he'd known them for months. This right here was an amazing sight. He'd come such a long way with his self-confidence, and an even longer way in his acceptance of family. It left me almost reeling to know that he was already offering comfort to Leilani, to our future daughter—no, not future, she was already ours. Seeing him hug her was a wonderful thing, and warmth bloomed in my chest at the sight. They were fucking beautiful.

Seb caught my eye, but only to roll his at me and shake his head a little. I suspected he wanted to flip me off or call me an asshole for being so sappy, but he somehow refrained.

I don't want to call you an asshole. Or I hadn't before you thought it.

I snorted at him, then closed my eyes and hugged the four-year-old tighter. Mother of All, I wished we could take them home today.

I never thought leaving this place would be so difficult. I don't want them to spend another moment off coven land. Seb's thoughts mirrored my own.

If we take them with us, we'll be charged with kidnapping, and while I doubt they'd arrest us, it could make it harder to adopt them legally. Being Sage and having a hand in stopping the war, not to mention helping the government, had its benefits, but that wasn't something I wanted to test when it came to our new kids.

Seb sighed inside my head. *I know. I hate this.*

Me too, but we'll bring them home as soon as we're allowed.

Okay.

After a moment, I said through our link, *Sebastian.*

Ailin.

Thank you for this.

He huffed out loud and shot me a glare. *You don't need to thank me, asshole. For fuck's sake.*

I couldn't help but chuckle out loud. "There it is."

He rolled his eyes.

At this point, every time he called me an asshole, it was with affection and more of an endearment than anything else. So I purposefully tried to get it out of him, and it never failed to make me smirk. Which was probably not the reaction he wanted, but he'd have to deal with it.

After the girls pulled out of our arms, Seb asked them a few questions, like what their favorite colors were and what type of art supplies they liked. At first, I thought he was simply trying to get to know them better, but I soon realized he was cataloguing everything so we could buy them everything they liked for our home. And that made me smirk at him more than before. He flat out ignored me.

Then I had a thought. "Girls?" They both turned their attention to me. "I wanted to let you know that we're also adopting one other child."

Leilani's eyes went wide, but Niya only continued to stare, then blurted, "Who?"

"Remington, the six-month-old human? We're adopting him as well."

Leilani said, "You're getting a baby, too?"

"Yes," I said. "You two and Remi. As soon as all the paperwork is set, we'll be back here to take all three of you home."

Leilani was frowning slightly, but Niya smiled. "I'm gonna have a baby brother?"

Seb chuckled. "Yes, sweetie, you are."

Niya bounced on her toes and giggled, so I ruffled her hair, then checked the time. We needed to head out before they kicked us out for their dinner rush.

I sighed, and Seb frowned but nodded in understanding as I said, "We have to get going, girls. We'll be back as soon as we can, okay?"

Leilani nodded, her gaze going to the floor, and Niya let out the most dramatic sigh I'd ever heard—I had to hold in a laugh, because we were probably in trouble with that one—and said, "Guess we gotta go eat dinner." It was crazy we'd been here so long it was almost dinnertime.

Seb held back a smile and said, "Guess you do. We'll see you soon, okay? And if… if you two need something before we come to pick you up, tell Mrs. Hunley to call us, okay? We'll come right over if you need anything."

My chest warmed toward my viramore again, but I nodded to the girls. "He's right. I'll tell Mrs. Hunley myself that you two can call us anytime you want, okay?"

They both nodded, Niya grinning at us.

Saying goodbye was kind of horrible, but knowing we'd be back to bring them home next time helped ease the ache and the protective instincts I had toward the girls and Remi. I gave them each a hug and a kiss on the temple, and Seb did the same before we reluctantly walked out.

Seb was moving slowly, so I said, "After we talk to Mrs. Hunley, let's go figure out everything we need to buy for the three of them. We can redo their rooms and buy clothes—Mrs. Hunley should know their sizes—and get them art supplies and everything else you found out they liked."

He nodded and wiped his eye. "I don't want to leave any of them here."

"I know, but we don't have a choice right now."

He nodded and let me lead him out of the room, down the hall, and straight to Mrs. Hunley's office.

I knocked on her open door, and when she looked at me, I said, "We're heading out, but we wanted to know if you have their clothes sizes?"

"Oh, yes, of course." She shuffled some papers around, then opened her laptop, and a minute later, she was passing me a piece of paper with their sizes written down.

"Thank you."

"Of course." She chewed her inner lip nervously, so I waited a minute for her to say what she needed to say. "Have you heard anything about the Brinnswick Union pulling our funding?"

My eyes widened. "No, I haven't. What the hell? Why would they do that?"

She shrugged, looking helpless. "I'm not sure, but I've heard it from more than one person in some of our outreach programs."

I ran a hand over my face, then made eye contact with her. "I'll see what I can find out. Don't worry about it, I'm not going to let that happen." Not if I had any say in it.

She gave me a nod of thanks, and Seb and I headed out.

Seb added in my head, *They better not pull the funding or I'll kick their asses.*

That made me grin. My viramore was kind and sweet and seemed like he wouldn't hurt a fly, but he was fierce as hell when he was fighting enemies or sticking up for his family. If those fucking representative assholes on the Union board wanted to pull funds, they were going to have to deal with my viramore and me. I didn't think that was something they'd want to deal with.

Seb nudged me. *You can't just blast them, even if they deserve it. Assholes.*

No, but threatening them should be enough.

Seb snorted his amusement.

I said, "Let's not think about that right now; we just adopted three kids. We. Adopted. Three. Children."

He smiled. "I know."

I pecked his lips and led him out the front doors. Once we were in the car, Seb's Bonded dragon Zammerra pulled herself to Seb and popped up right on his lap. She was in her small form, so she looked like a baby dragon even though she was over four years old. Her purple and black scales sparkled in the sunlight streaming in through the windshield, and her knowing eyes were wiser than her age. Seb Bonded with her after his experiences with the elder ogre before the Berserker War had truly started, so the young dragon had seen a lot in her short lifetime. Being a Bonded, she was able to use her Bond with Sebastian to pull herself to him, no matter where or how far he was from her, and Seb could do the same. She could also change her form and size, although she typically stuck to her small size so she could curl around Seb's neck or sit on his lap.

My Bonded was a manticore that preferred being in the form of a black cat or kitten. She also loved curling up on Seb's lap, although both the dragon and cat loved hanging all over me as well... sometimes. Zammerra and Seraphina were the best of friends now, although there were times when Sera behaved as if Zamm was her baby. I suppose that was natural since Zamm had been a baby when Seb had found her.

"You alright, baby?" I asked Seb.

He sighed. "Yeah."

I leaned over the console to kiss his cheek, but Seb turned to me so I kissed his lips instead. Since I was at an awkward angle, and we were still in front of the orphanage, I only lingered against his lips for a few seconds. Once I settled in my seat, I put the car in *drive* and said, "Aspen has all the baby stuff that didn't get ruined in the… that night." Seb knew I meant the night my parents and half of our coven were slaughtered. I didn't talk about it, and I didn't want to think about it. I'd told Seb everything I remembered about that night long ago, so I didn't need to rehash it for him.

"Do you want to buy stuff? Or should we make things at home?" he asked without missing a beat—knowing what I needed, as always.

I sighed. "We probably need to buy things. We can have a crib and beds and dressers and stuff made with the trees, I think, but there are other things we might need for a baby. Plus, diapers and all that. Let's go to a store and see if the people there can help us figure out what the hell we need. We're going to end up buying the whole damn store, but whatever."

When I glanced at him, he smiled softly. "Okay."

The happiness I felt coming from him made my anxiety over this new venture ease. He was excited about bringing these kids into our home—our kids. He didn't feel as if I was pressuring him, he truly wanted this as badly as I did.

Reaching over with one hand while steering with the other, I squeezed his thigh. He settled his hand over mine, and I grinned.

BY THE TIME WE GOT HOME, WE'D BASICALLY BURNED A HOLE IN MY pocket by buying absolutely everything you could imagine for a baby, a four-year-old, and an eleven-year-old, and we were both exhausted.

Luckily for us, one of my older kids—my nineteen-year-old Tio—was cooking up a huge dinner.

All of my adult-aged children still lived on coven land, but in their own houses instead of with me. But Seb and I lived in "the big house" where the kids were in and out, and everyone met for dinner whenever they could. There were so many people in my coven now that whoever was cooking made enough food to feed an army, but even when there were leftovers, they got eaten within a day or two. The family was always welcome inside our home, even if they only came to forage for food in the fridge. That was their favorite pastime, apparently. Especially when Tio was the one that cooked—our resident chef.

"What's all that?" Tio asked from the kitchen doorway.

Seb turned to me to answer, so I smiled at Tiordan and said, "We're adopting three kids."

Tio blinked at me a few times, then let out a laugh. "Guess Jor is winning the bet."

"What bet?"

Tio shrugged. "We all took bets on when you guys were going to adopt more kids, and I'm pretty sure he's the closest, so he wins the prize."

"You guys took bets?" Seb asked in disbelief.

Tio grinned. "Duh. We knew Dad was going to convince you eventually."

I snorted and shook my head.

Tio asked, "How many kids are you adopting?"

"Three," I answered.

He grinned. "I can't remember who had three kids. I had you down for four."

Seb opened and closed his mouth, then a laugh bubbled out as he asked, "Are you kidding me, Tio? You had a fucking side bet going on, too?"

"Yep." He didn't even look ashamed.

I pointed at him. "Little shits, all of you."

He chuckled as he walked back into the kitchen. "Dinner will be done in a half hour."

"Thank you for cooking, kiddo!" I yelled back.

"Yeah, yeah."

I grinned and met Seb's eyes. "Let's get this shit upstairs."

He nodded and followed, but grumbled the entire time. "I can't believe they placed bets!"

"Is it really that surprising?"

"I've been saying I didn't want more kids because we have enough. Why would they all assume we'd adopt more?"

I looked over my shoulder at him with a smirk. "Really? Like you didn't know deep down that we'd bring more kids into our family."

He sighed. "I must be really predictable."

"Only a little."

"Don't humor me, A."

Since I didn't want him getting more pissy with me, I didn't respond to that, even if I wanted to tell him I liked humoring him.

"I heard that, asshole."

Shit. "Sorry."

"No, you're not."

I snorted as I pushed open one of the kids' old bedrooms that was directly across from my and Seb's room. It used to be Jorah's room. As I set the bags down, I sighed, and when Seb put his arm around me, I leaned back into him. "I can't believe my little boy has a house of his own now."

Seb kissed my hair. "Me either, but at least he's only down the path."

"I know. It's not the same, though."

"No, it's not." He kissed me again before walking to the bags to peek inside. "Who do you want to put in this room? Remi?"

"Yeah, I think so. And maybe put Niya in the next one over and Leilani in the one beside that."

"All of them on the other side of the hall?" He meant from our room.

I shrugged. "I don't have a preference except for being closer to the baby, and maybe Niya. She's older, but nightmares are still a thing."

"That works for me. Let's grab all the crap out of the car, and we can separate everything into the right rooms afterward."

Before he could get too far down the hall, I grabbed him and pushed him against the wall, going up on my toes to claim his mouth. I buried one hand in his hair and slipped the other under his shirt to touch his soft, golden-brown skin. Before my cock got too excited, I pulled back and smirked at his blown pupils. "Couldn't resist, baby." I kissed him quickly. "Not even sorry."

Before I could walk away, he grabbed hold of my waist and yanked me into his body as he reclaimed my lips in a bruising kiss. He began walking me backward, and I didn't pay attention to where he was leading me until I heard the bedroom door shut behind him. He reached down and grabbed the backs of my thighs to lift me into his arms, and I smiled against his lips as I hooked my legs around his waist and my arms around his neck.

What are you planning to do to me, detective? I asked as I rutted against him.

Fuck you. Obviously.

I snorted and buried my hands in his hair. Sometimes it still surprised me when he said things like that. My sweet, shy, easily embarrassed detective had come a long way.

I broke our kiss, but only to mutter a spell that made our clothes disappear. As soon as our skin rubbed together, I shivered.

"I love that you can do that," Seb whispered, lowering me down to the bed and kissing along my throat.

I grunted in agreement. "We don't have fucking time, Seb. You need to fuck me right now."

He groaned. "No one will care if we're late for dinner, A." I lifted a brow at him, and he groaned again. "Fine." He whispered a spell, and lube formed in his hand. I watched him slather his gorgeous cock with it, then he grinned at me as he slid a lubed finger inside my entrance.

When he leaned down to suck on my nipple, I moaned loudly and arched into him. "Mm. Fuck, baby, so good," I said.

He licked down my stomach and added a second finger. Seb had fucked me into the mattress last night, so it wouldn't take much prep for me to be ready for him. Before I could voice that out loud, he licked a stripe up my cock and put the tip between his plump lips, swirling his tongue around.

I moaned, and he took me deep into his throat. "Fuck, baby. Fuck, fuck, fuck."

He bobbed up and down as he added a third finger and brushed my prostate, and for a second, I was afraid I was going to come down his throat. But I didn't want to come yet.

I pushed his shoulder to get him to release me, and when he looked up at me with those honey eyes I loved so much and his pink cheeks flushed with lust, he took my breath away for a moment. I sucked in a deep breath and said, "I need you inside me, Seb."

He smiled and leaned up to kiss my lips. He pulled out his fingers, and I almost whimpered, but he kissed me so thoroughly I was distracted for a moment. He deepened the kiss as I dug my fingers in his hair again, and I felt his love and affection for me expand through our link. My chest tightened and warmed as my magic swirled outside my body. The instant my green magic exploded out, Seb's blue magic escaped him to join in. Even with my eyes closed, I knew our magics were swirling around in a sweet waltz together; I could feel it.

"Ailin," Seb whimpered against my lips.

"I'm right here, baby." Wrapping my arms around his back, I pulled him closer. "Please…"

He didn't have to ask what I wanted; he could sense it through our connection. Seb lined his cock up and slowly slipped inside, pausing to let me adjust. He rained kisses down over my face and neck, and I pressed my ass back so he'd slide in farther.

Once he was fully seated, I groaned and looked up at him. He was leaning on his elbows on either side of my head, carding his fingers through my hair and staring at me with those sweet eyes filled with lust. Behind him, our magics danced and swirled, our souls happy to be together.

Leaning my head up, I kissed him, and when I fell back, he brought his mouth with me. His tongue pried my mouth open as he slowly pulled out and just as slowly pushed back in. He kept a slow, steady, and deep as hell pace that had me quivering beneath him. When he broke our kiss, I grabbed his head and pulled his lips back, making him smile against me.

I started getting frustrated because I wanted him to go faster, and I knew he was doing it on purpose to make me crazy. "Pick up the pace."

"Nope."

I panted out, "Don't start... an argument... when you're... fucking me."

"I wasn't."

"Yes, you were."

"I didn't start it."

I groaned in frustration—and in pleasure—then wrapped my legs and arms tight around him. With the help of my magic, I rolled him onto his back without letting go, and he laughed and kissed me. He braced his feet on the bed to thrust up into me as I picked up the pace. He moaned beneath me, and I grabbed his hands, laced our fingers together, and put them over his head before leaning down to suck a bruise over his vitmea mark.

He moaned, "Ailin," and squeezed our hands tighter.

I squeezed back. "Right here, baby."

"Fuck," he cried out, so close to orgasming.

Feeling his big cock brushing my prostate with every stroke and hearing all his little moans and whimpers had me ready to explode. I pulled his earlobe between my teeth and breathlessly said, "Let go, baby... I'll be right here to catch you." I sucked on his vitmea mark again.

He cried out as his cock emptied into me, and feeling his pleasure through our link set off my own orgasm. My cum hit our stomachs and chests as he filled me up, green and blue light encompassed my vision, every cell in my body was overcome with pleasure that kept going and going, making me cry out again and again.

When it finally stopped, I was spent and collapsed on top of him, our fingers still tangled together. Seb's chest was rising and falling as he tried to catch his breath, and even though I knew I was squishing him, he didn't want me to move and I sure as hell didn't want to either.

Connecting like this was almost like a dream. We were always connected, always able to communicate, to sense what the other person was feeling. But when we brought our bodies together, when we concentrated on only each other and our connection, the love we felt for one another shined through and became all-encompassing. Every piece of my soul intertwined with his, our hearts beat as one, I could feel him in every inch of my skin.

Seb unlaced our fingers, but only so he could wrap his arms around me and kiss my forehead. I remained listless on top of him, but he didn't mind. Eventually, he rolled us to our sides, but he kept our bodies flat against each other, hugging me to him.

Our magics were still floating around us, but as we came back to ourselves, they slowed and began to fade.

"Thank you," I breathed a few minutes later.

He laughed. "Did you seriously just thank me for having sex?"

I chuckled. "No, you idiot. I thanked you for... for adopting the kids with me."

He ran his fingers through the non-braided side of my hair and kissed my forehead. "You don't have to thank me for that, A. I should be the one thanking you."

My brow furrowed. "What the hell for?"

He snorted. "You gave me a family, showed me what it meant to love and be loved, and now you're bringing even more of that into our lives. Not only that, but we're going to show those three kids what it means to be a part of our family and what it means to be loved unconditionally."

Leaning up a little, I kissed his vitmea mark. "You've shown me those things, too, you know."

"Yeah right. You had a huge family before we ever met. You've had a huge family your entire life."

I nodded and tilted my head up to meet his eyes. "Maybe, but I didn't have a viramore before you. What we have is... eternal, endless. And it grows every day that you're with me."

He stared at me for several seconds, then shook his head. "Sometimes I wonder how you've fooled so many people into thinking you're this total badass jerk."

"I am a total badass, you jerk."

He snorted. "You are, but you're kinda a huge romantic that I don't know what to do with sometimes."

I lifted a brow at him.

He sighed and rolled a little, moving me until we were sharing a pillow and facing each other. "I feel it too, you know."

That made me smile. "I know."

"I didn't think it was possible to love someone like this, let alone for it to happen to me. Growing up, I... I didn't have anyone."

"I know," I whispered.

"And now I have everything, *and* I have you. It's... if someone would've told me when I was a kid that I'd have a huge family and a guy that loves me more than I thought possible, I would've never believed it. That place, Eastbrook Youth Academy, it was a bad place to grow up. Love wasn't something that was accepted there, and definitely not something we were given."

Every time he talked about his childhood, it made me cringe and wish I could go back in time to take out all those assholes that used to run the orphanage. The orphanage that was basically used to create soldiers. Mindless, loveless soldiers. It was fucking terrible, and I hated that he'd grown up that way. If I could, I'd hunt down every asshole that locked him in isolation, every dickhead that laid a hand on him. They deserved to be taken out... slowly.

"Hey."

Seb's voice made me focus on him.

He offered a sad smile. "You don't have to be upset for me anymore, A."

I sighed. "I hate that you went through that. Those people used to lock you in the damn closet because you were having nightmares, they slapped your wrists whenever they felt like it, and did all kinds of shitty things to you. Withheld food, kept you isolated from the others, made you feel like you were worthless. I'm allowed to be pissed about that, Sebastian. If I could, I'd hunt those bastards down and make them suffer the way you did. They deserve a slow death for abusing kids like that."

Seb placed his hand on my cheek. "Your magic is floating off of you, sweetheart. Calm down."

I closed my eyes and took a deep breath. I didn't exactly want to calm down, but I also didn't want to upset my viramore, so I kept taking calming breaths until I felt like I was in control. When I opened my eyes, I was met with Seb's concerned eyes. "I'm fucking fine," I ground out.

He chuckled. "You sound like it."

"Whatever."

He pecked my lips. "We need to get to dinner."

I sighed. "Yeah."

"Hey, Ailin?"

"Hey, Sebastian."

"You don't have to worry about any of that shit that happened to me. It's in the past, and… and I'd do it all over again if it meant my life would lead to you. I wouldn't change a thing."

My throat clogged with emotion, so I leaned in to press my lips to his in a lingering kiss. No tongue, just lips to lips, and I pushed my love for him through our link so he'd feel what it meant. Seb pushed his love for me right back, and I almost gasped at the enormity of it.

When we pulled away, his cheeks were flushed and he shot me a shy smile.

After one more peck to the lips, I muttered the spell to clean and re-dress us, and we headed downstairs for dinner. I'd tell any of the kids that were here tonight about our adoption plans, but I was going to have to call a few of them. I knew Delaro was with his two viramores—Nikolai and Grayson—right now, so he wouldn't be here tonight. I sighed to myself. Of all the people in the world, one of Delaro's viramores had to be Nikolai. Fucking fae asshole.

I rubbed my forehead as we walked down the steps.

"You need to give the guy a chance," Seb said from behind me.

"I've been fucking nice to him, haven't I?"

Seb cringed, and I rolled my eyes.

"I'll do better. Fuck."

Seb chuckled as we stepped off the landing. "We still have plenty of kids that need to meet their viramores, or even just date. You better get used to it."

"For fuck's sake, Sebastian, I don't want to think about it."

He laughed and walked over to the table that already had ten people sitting at it.

Tiordan grinned at me. "All the food's already on the table, Dad."

"Thanks, Tio," I said, taking my seat beside Seb.

Jorah, my youngest—before today—sat on my other side and offered a grin. "Thanks for making me win."

I snorted. "Unbelievable."

"When do we get to meet our new siblings?" Jorah asked with a smile.

The fact that all the kids here tonight seemed to already know didn't surprise me. Tio probably called them as soon as Seb and I went upstairs. But the fact that they were all smiling and waiting for my answer made something inside of me settle. They were happy Seb and I were bringing more people into our family. Not that I'd thought they wouldn't be, but knowing they'd be alright was different. Still, I said, "You know this doesn't mean we love you any less, right?"

I got a whole lot of eye rolls and groans. Seb chuckled, but I could tell he was as relieved by their reaction as I was.

Tio said, "Damn, Dad, like you even have to say that."

I cleared my throat. "Sorry, I needed to make that clear."

They all groaned again, and Jorah said, "Duh." He waved me off. "When are they coming home?"

I sent them each an appreciative smile, then said, "We're not sure, but hopefully it won't be more than a week."

"I can't wait. What are their names?" Clover asked, my youngest girl—again, until today.

Seb smiled at me before answering her, and we spent the rest of dinner telling the kids about Leilani, Niya, and Remi.

CHAPTER THREE

SEBASTIAN

I was nervous as hell walking into Eastbrook Youth Academy for the second time in the last twenty-three years. But this time it wasn't nerves about being in the terrible place I grew up in—okay, maybe there was a little bit of that too, but it was overshadowed—I was nervous about seeing the kids again and bringing them home. We were going to be responsible for the lives and well-being of three little people. Three people were going to count on us for everything.

We've taken care of our other kids, Seb. There's nothing to be nervous about. Ailin's words were calm, but he couldn't fool me. He was nervous, too. Excited, yes, but there was some nervousness coming from him as well. *Maybe your nerves are rubbing off on me.*

You can rub off on me later.

He gaped at me for a second before laughing and pushing my shoulder. "Let's go get our kids."

I nodded and followed him inside.

Mrs. Hunley was waiting for us in the foyer this time, and she smiled widely as we walked in. After greeting us, she waved a hand toward the room where she'd been reading kids stories the other day and said, "They're waiting for you inside. They already have their things packed up."

Ailin said, "Thank you." To me, he held out a hand that I took instantly and said, "Ready?"

"No. Yes. Probably."

He chuckled and pulled me to the door. I squeezed his hand as he opened it, and when it swung open revealing Niya hopping around the room, Leilani sketching in a sketch pad on her lap, and Remi being swung in a baby swing, I took a breath and smiled. Releasing Ailin's hand, I walked in ahead of him and said, "Hey, guys."

Niya stopped hopping and turned big, excited eyes to me, then ran over and threw her arms around my waist, screaming, "Hi!"

I chuckled and hugged her back. "Hey, Niya, how are you today?"

"I'm great!" she yelled louder than necessary. "Are you really taking us home with you?"

"We are." I nodded.

"Even that baby?"

I snorted. "Yes, even that baby. His name's Remi, by the way."

"I know. He's kinda cute, but has smelly poops."

I laughed, and Leilani chastised, "Niya, what did I tell you about that?"

I opened my mouth to tell Leilani it was okay, but Ailin's subtle shake of his head gave me pause. In my head, he said, *She's used to looking out for her; don't step on her toes. Not right now.* He was standing beside Leilani, obviously having greeted her while I'd greeted Niya.

I gave him a nod of understanding.

Niya rolled her eyes. "Not to talk about poops."

"Exactly," Leilani said, then turned bright red as she glanced between Ailin and me.

Ailin moved in and rubbed her back, whispering something to her, so I figured he had it handled and tilted my head down to speak to Niya. "Do you want to help me get the little stinker out of his swing?"

She giggled and threw a fist in the air, almost knocking me out in the process, then ran over to Remi. I quickly followed so she didn't try getting him out on her own. It took me a minute to figure out how to stop the swing, and then another couple of minutes to figure out how the hell to undo the straps. Finally, I pulled Remi out of the swing, and he smiled at me and smacked my cheek with his little fist. That made Niya giggle.

Kneeling down, I turned Remi so his back was to my chest and he was facing Niya, his new sister. He gurgled at her, and she giggled again and patted his head gently. For such a hyper girl, I'd been afraid she'd be too rough with Remi, but she was surprisingly gentle. At least right now. Who the hell knew what she'd be like once they were used to each other?

Ailin came over, hugged Niya, and kissed the top of Remi's head. I passed Ailin the baby—it was pretty awkward, but we'd have to get used to it—then walked over to Leilani. She seemed shy and unsure, and since I knew how that felt, I took the initiative. I very slowly pulled her into a hug, giving her plenty of time to back away. Once my arms were around her shoulders, she hugged me back and sank into me.

She hugged me for such a long time, I was worried that she hadn't had a good hug in a while. And that broke my heart. I knew she'd been old enough to remember losing her parents in the war.

Leilani and Niya's human father had apparently been on the front lines, so for all I knew, I'd run into him before he was killed in action. Their nymph mother had died in one of the many explosions the berserkers set off. They had been hiding in their house, and when the fighting got close, their mother had hidden them under the staircase. An explosion took out part of their home, and their mother had died covering them with her body.

When Ailin had told me their story, my heart ached, and now that I had this little girl in my arms, it throbbed. Niya had only been a year old when it happened, so she—luckily—didn't have any memories of it. But Leilani had been seven years old, and according to the therapist here, she remembered the explosion. Therapy was something we were going to continue, if she and the doctor thought she needed it. This poor little girl had already been through way too much.

She must've felt so lonely after losing her parents only a few weeks apart. Even having her sister, she clearly felt responsible for her, which meant Leilani was growing up way too fast. We were going to have to show her what it was like to be a kid again, show her that Ailin and I were here and that we'd take care of Niya so she didn't have to. But that was going to take a lot of trust, and trust took time to build. It was going to be a long road, but as long as Ailin and I made sure all three of them knew we were here for them and that we loved them—because even a few hours with them already solidified that, and I knew it would grow every day—I knew we'd all be okay.

We broke apart, and I noticed that Mrs. Hunley was standing in the doorway watching us with tears in her eyes. She smiled at me and gave me a nod of appreciation that I returned. She was truly doing a marvelous job here with all these kids.

Ailin asked, "Are you guys ready to come see your new home?"

Leilani and Niya exchanged a look before the both nodded at him. Niya put on her backpack, Leilani picked up two bags, and I picked up the bag that had Remi's name on it. Niya grabbed my hand, Ailin shifted Remi in his arms, and when he began walking, the girls and I followed him out.

Mrs. Hunley handed me a huge-ass folder with about a million papers in it, said goodbye to the kids and us, and waved us out the door.

When Ailin was getting Remi into the car seat we'd installed the other day and the girls were climbing in on the other side of the SUV, it hit me that we were really taking them home with us.

Ailin shot me a little smirk before he kissed Remi's temple and walked around the car to get into the driver's seat. I threw all the bags in the trunk. We'd talked earlier about who was driving us home and I voted for him because I was too nervous. It was one thing driving myself or Ailin or the older kids, it was an entirely different thing thinking about driving two little girls and a baby. Nope. No thank you. Not until I was used to the responsibility of having them.

Everyone was quiet for a minute, but Ailin finally asked, "Did you guys have lunch yet?"

Niya answered, "Nope. Just reakfast."

I hid a smile at that... *reakfast*, so cute.

Ailin grinned. "Good. Tiordan made a bunch of food last night to prepare for you guys coming home. He's one of… well, he's one of my kids, so he's your brother." *Is that weird to say to them?*

I have no idea, A. I'm fucking clueless right now.

Don't freak out.

I'm not.

Yes, you are. Out loud he said, "Anyway, I told you guys before that I have a lot of kids, so you guys are going to have a bunch of siblings. They're all older and have moved out of the house. They still live on coven land, so they're within walking distance." He cringed. *I'm giving them too much fucking information, aren't I? Fuck.*

Hell if I know. I turned in my seat to find Niya staring out the window and Leilani staring at her hands in her lap. Clearing my throat, I said, "Don't worry, none of the other kids are coming to the house today. We're going to let you guys settle in and meet them in small numbers, okay?"

Leilani shrugged, and Niya said, "'Kay!" She was a loud, loud kid.

I said, "Just so you know, they're all really excited to meet you. They even planned a family party to welcome you three home, but we're making them wait until next week to throw it. Is that… is that okay with you?"

"A party?" Niya's eyes were wide.

I nodded. "Yes, a party. Just the family, but there's a lot of us Ellwoods."

Niya grinned, and Leilani said, "That's cool."

I figured that was as good as I was going to get, so I turned back in my seat. Ailin reached over and squeezed my thigh before putting both hands back on the steering wheel. I heard him think, *I could use a joint.*

I turned sharply to him. "Don't you dare with them in the car."

He rolled his eyes. "I wasn't planning to, Sebastian." He sounded exasperated.

"You better not."

"I won't."

"Ever."

He paused and glanced at me for a split-second. "Not with the kids in the car." *For fuck's sake, Sebastian, I would never do that. Ass.*

Crossing my arms over my chest, I huffed. He had a habit of smoking in my car when I was driving and he was stressed. I used to hate it, but I actually didn't really mind anymore. But not around the kids.

I would never fucking do that.

I know. And now I hurt his feelings. *I know you wouldn't. My nerves are just frazzled. I'm sorry.*

He nodded.

Don't be mad.

"I'm not, baby," he whispered. *I'm on edge. I'll be better when we get them on coven land.*

Same here.

It wasn't long before we passed through our warded barrier and onto the Ellwood property. Ailin had added Niya, Leilani, and Remi to the wards a few days ago, so there was no issue with driving straight over the bridge and up the driveway to the big house. When we turned the corner, I heard Leilani gasp.

I couldn't blame her. I was pretty sure I gasped the first time I saw the big house, too.

The big house was a huge mansion that was made out of trees like something out of a fairytale. The trees were still living and had grown and shaped their branches to form a huge home with windows and doors and different rooms and floors. It was actually a little insane looking if you weren't expecting it. Insane and beautiful, like nothing else in our world, to be honest. Well, now there were several other smaller homes built the same way on the property that the older kids lived in, but nowhere outside of the Ellwood coven land had I ever seen anything quite like it.

"Are those really trees?" Leilani asked. "I can feel them... you live in a huge living tree house."

"We do," Ailin said with a smile.

I glanced at Leilani and Niya and noticed the same expression of awe on their faces. Their nymph halves would appreciate living in trees like this and being closer to nature. Or at least I hoped they would.

Ailin parked the car and the two of us got out. I went straight over to Remi, pulling him out of the complicated car seat—that was going to take some getting used to—and Ailin opened the door for the girls, who climbed out, still staring at the house in awe. My viramore passed the girls their bags from the trunk, then took Remi's bag since I was carrying him.

"Let's go inside," Ailin said, leading the girls to the front porch with Remi and me right behind them.

Ailin gave them a tour of the first floor, and they were all quiet, then he asked, "Would you like to see your rooms before we eat?"

"Yes!" Niya yelled while Leilani nodded and Remi giggled as Ailin poked his belly.

As we climbed the stairs, I said, "If you guys don't like what we did with the rooms, we can change them, and if you decide you want a different room than the ones we gave you, that's fine, too. We can move things around to make it comfortable for you."

Halfway down the hall, Ailin stopped at a door, saying, "Leilani, this one's for you. Niya's right next door, and Remi's on the other side of her."

Leilani froze and stared at Ailin for a long moment. "Wait, we're getting our own rooms?"

Without missing a beat, Ailin said, "Yes. You can share if you want, or sleep in each other's rooms if that makes you more comfortable, but you each have your own room, your own space."

She blinked at him for a while before giving a slight nod and stepping into the room. She'd told me her favorite color was blue, so we painted the walls blue and picked out bedding and curtains to match it.

I bounced Remi in my arms and said, "We didn't hang anything on the walls because we wanted you to be able to decorate it, if you want. If you don't like that color, we can change it, no problem, and—"

"I love it," she said, cutting me off. "I really love it." She faced us with watery eyes. "Thank you."

"You're welcome, kiddo," Ailin said, giving her a little side-hug and a kiss on the temple. I gave her a side-hug as well, and Ailin asked, "Want to see yours, Niya?"

"Yes!"

I chuckled and followed them with Leilani beside me. The poor eleven-year-old was obviously stressed and overwhelmed.

Ailin opened Niya's bedroom door, and the little girl gasped loudly. It was painted in purples and light grays with prince and princess superheroes all over the walls. Finding that combination had been difficult, so we'd had to use a little magic.

"Princess superheroes!" Niya yelled before flying into the room and examining everything up close.

"How did you find that?" Leilani asked.

"We bought some prince and princess stuff and some superhero stuff, and some of the other kids helped us combine them together. Well, I didn't help because I didn't know what to do, but Jorah and Delaro worked together to create some crazy weaving spell, I dunno. But it turned out great, right?"

Leilani smiled and nodded. "She loves it."

I watched the four-year-old move from place to place with an ear-splitting grin on her face and was extremely happy that we'd taken the time to figure out how to combine two of her favorite things.

Niya found a prince superhero that was wearing a crooked crown with a mask covering his eyes, and she giggled at the wall decal. It was adorable.

We gave her a few minutes before we all walked to Remi's room. His room was colorful with blues and pinks and greens all over. There was a huge pile of stuffed animals in the corner that Niya immediately ran over and dive bombed into. Remi of course, was more interested in pulling my hair than staring at the room, but Ailin picked up one of the many chewy things we'd bought and handed it over to the little guy. Remi grabbed it, fascinated, and let go of my hair as he shoved the toy in his mouth.

"Thank you," I mumbled.

"Anytime, baby."

I flicked Ailin's cheek before walking out of the room and saying, "Anyone else hungry? I'm starving, and I think I need to feed Remi before he starts eating my hair again."

The whole group followed me downstairs.

Lunch was a quiet affair, and I honestly couldn't remember the last time a meal had been so quiet in this house. There were always a million people coming in and out, and the Ellwoods were all loud. Well, most of them, anyway. I supposed growing up in a family this big, you'd have to be loud to be heard. Apparently, I'd gotten used to this craziness, too, because this was almost *too* quiet.

Ailin cleared his throat and asked, "Do you guys want to play a game when you finish eating?"

"What kind of game?" Leilani asked. She was being subdued, but she didn't seem quite as uncomfortable now that we'd been here for a few hours.

Ailin shrugged. "Some kind of board game, I guess? Or cards. We have a ton of stuff in the closet in the hall. You two can pick out something."

Leilani nodded, and Niya said, "Go Fish!"

"That's a baby game. They don't want to play Go Fish, Niya," Leilani said.

Ailin smiled at them. "We don't mind that, kiddo. Go Fish sounds fun to me."

Leilani shot him a look of disbelief before shrugging her shoulders and staring at her plate, and Niya gave Ailin a huge grin.

We ended up moving into the living room to play because Remi was still drinking his bottle, and he was falling asleep in my arms, so Ailin wanted me to be more comfortable. With my arm on a pillow and a baby cradled against me, I played Go Fish with Niya, Leilani, and Ailin for almost an entire hour before Leilani didn't want to play anymore.

Ailin took the cards and started teaching the girls some strange witch card game that was complicated and weird, but sort of like Slap Jack and Rummy combined... kinda. I wasn't sure if he was just making up rules as he went to make the girls laugh, or if the rules were really that odd, but he was so happy, I didn't care either way.

He sent me a wink at that, but didn't miss a beat with the game.

Dinner wasn't quite so quiet since now that Niya was more comfortable in the house, she was back to her normal, loud self. She spoke very clearly for being so young—or maybe my judgment was off, I dunno—but I suppose that was due to the fact that she never stopped talking.

By the time we were all ready for bed, we were exhausted. I didn't want to put Remi in his crib because I wanted to keep him close, but I did anyway, if only so I could give the girls each a proper hug good night.

Niya hugged me tight, and I whispered against her hair, "We'll be right across the hall if you need us. Our door will be open." We'd pointed out which room was ours earlier and decided to keep the door open so we'd hear them if they needed us, and to show we meant it when we said they could come to us if they needed something.

"Okay. Good night, Seb," she said.

I kissed her hair. "Good night, pumpkin."

She giggled and lay back so I could cover her. After a kiss to her forehead, I walked out of the room, passing Ailin on the way. He'd been saying good night to Leilani. He kissed my cheek along the way before going into Niya's room as I went into Leilani's. She was sitting up on the edge of the bed, looking a little nervous.

I sat beside her, giving her some space, and asked, "Do you need anything else before bed?"

She shook her head. "No, thank you."

I hesitated, then took a breath and said, "It's okay if you say no, I promise I won't be mad at you or upset in any way, but... can I give you a hug?"

That made her snap her head up and shoot me a shy smile before she nodded. I scooted over and gently pulled her into my side to give her a little hug. Like earlier, she surprised me by leaning into me and relaxing.

"You know we're across the hall if you need us, right?" She nodded, so I added, "And if you don't want to stay in here by yourself, you can go into Niya's room, or hell, our room, if you want. It's up to you, okay? I know it's a strange place that doesn't feel like home yet, and we just want you to be comfortable, okay?"

"Okay… thanks."

I kissed the top of her head before releasing her and standing up. "If you lay down, I'll tuck you in." She wasn't too old for that, was she?

She hesitated before nodding and scooting up on her bed.

I pulled the blankets up over her and offered a smile. "We're right across the hall if you need us, sweetie."

She nodded.

I started to head out of the room before pausing and turning back to face her. "Leilani?"

"Yeah?"

"I just thought you should know that… I grew up at Eastbrook Youth Academy."

Her eyes widened. "You did?"

I nodded. "Yeah, my whole life. I was left there when I was a baby and was never adopted, so I stayed until I was eighteen. So… I thought maybe you'd want to know that. You know, in case… well, I know how overwhelming it is to be brought into a family when you're not used to it. I was all alone until I was thirty-five when Ailin basically pulled me into his life and into the Ellwood family. If you have anything you want to talk about, I'm here, and if you ever feel over-whelmed with everything and you just need to get away from it, I promise that I'll understand. So will Ailin. That's one of the reasons we wanted you to have your own room. This is *your* space, okay? No one's coming in here unless you want them in here. Just… I'm here, and I wanted you to know."

She was quiet for a long minute, and I almost turned out the light and walked away to give her time to think about what I said, but her soft voice reached my ears. "I'm glad you finally found a family."

That made my eyes water. "Me too, sweetpea, and I'm so fucking happy that you're a part of it now." I cringed internally at the f-bomb drop, but I'd been good all day, so I'd call only one a win.

It made her chuckle. "Thanks… good night."

"Good night, Lani, we'll see you in the morning. Or you know, if you need us before then."

She giggled and waved at me as I turned off the light.

"Do you want the door shut, opened, or cracked?"

"Cracked please."

I nodded and pulled the door almost shut and turned around, finding Ailin in the hall, leaning one shoulder against the wall and smiling at me. I walked over to him, embracing him and bending a little to tuck my face against his neck, right on his vitmea mark.

We didn't need to say anything, it was enough to know that he was here.

When we parted, I checked on Remi one last time—he was still asleep—then went into our room, leaving the door half opened.

Despite being exhausted, it took me a long time to fall asleep. Ailin tucked himself against me, his face in my neck, his body draped half over mine, and he was out pretty quickly. We had a baby monitor for Remi, so I knew we'd wake up if he cried, but I was still worried that one of the kids was going to need us.

"Go to sleep, Sebastian," Ailin mumbled, scaring the shit out of me since I'd thought he was asleep. "How can I sleep with you thinking so loud?"

"Sorry."

"It's fine, just go the fuck to sleep already."

"I'm trying."

"No you're not. Count some goblins or whatever."

I snorted. "You mean count sheep?"

"Yeah, that."

"How the hell did you get goblins and sheep mixed up?"

He groaned. "They're basically the same thing."

"That's probably the most ridiculous thing you've ever said to me."

"Whatever. Goblins, sheep, what's the difference?"

I chuckled. "You're a dumbass."

"Go. To. Sleep. The baby will probably wake us up at some point, so sleep while you can."

I kissed his hair. "Alright, I'll try counting goblins."

He snorted. "Smart ass."

I chuckled and closed my eyes, settling in further. Instead of imagining sheep hopping a fence, I imagined goblins flipping over it, and I started counting.

"Lovely image," Ailin mumbled unintelligibly.

"You started it."

He sighed. "Sleep, or I'll hex you."

"You wouldn't dare."

He groaned. "Baby, stop talking."

I almost said that he was the one that wouldn't shut up, but I snapped my mouth closed.

"Sleep."

"Oh my god, A, if you'd stop telling me to sleep, I might actually be able to."

He chuckled against my neck and nuzzled me, placing a kiss on my vitmea mark and sending tingles through me.

"You're doing that on purpose, asshole, I know you are." He did it again, and the tingles spread. "Dammit, Ailin, I thought you wanted me to sleep?"

Instead of stopping, he kissed my skin again.

I sighed. "Stop it and go to sleep, asshat."

"Ugh, fine." He placed a few sloppy and wet kisses on my neck, making me squirm, before he settled in, and almost immediately, fell back to sleep.

Shaking my head, I kissed his hair and closed my eyes, counting damn goblins again.

Who would've thought it worked?

CHAPTER FOUR

AILIN

The kids had been home with us for three days, and I could no longer hold off on the party the older ones wanted to throw. All of my kids had come to meet their new little siblings one or two at a time, but they were determined to get the entire family together to celebrate bringing in new family members.

Niya was excited about it, and Leilani seemed indifferent, so as long as they were okay, I didn't mind. Plus, it was nice that the older kids wanted to make sure the little ones knew they were wanted here.

"How much longer?" Seb asked me.

"You know you have a phone, right? You could just look at the time," I replied.

He reached out his leg and nudged my knee with his toes. "Asshole. I'm holding the baby."

"You said a bad word," Niya sing-songed from her spot on the floor where she was playing with some toy cars.

"Sorry," Seb said with a cringe.

I smirked at him. "We should start a swear jar."

Leilani looked up from her sketchpad and said, "I'd be rich if we did that."

I couldn't help but chuckle.

Seb shrugged a shoulder and moved the baby a little. "You're worse than me."

"I've never held my tongue, and I don't plan on changing that. The rest of the kids turned out okay with me cursing all the time."

"They all have mouths on them," Seb said with a chuckle.

I lifted a shoulder and grinned.

Leilani said, "She's only saying that because no one was supposed to cuss at Eastbrook. I'll try to get her to stop yelling at you guys about it."

I waved that away. "It's fine, Lani. Neither of us mind. She'll get used to it eventually."

Leilani nodded, but bit her bottom lip. The poor kid seemed like she worried about everything. She was obviously used to keeping an eye on her sister, and while that was nice, we needed to prove to her that she didn't need to be Niya's parent anymore.

"Hello?" Tio's voice called from the back door.

"We're in the living room, Tio," I yelled back.

"Can I come in to get this shit in the oven?"

"You said a bad word!" Niya yelled, making everyone, even Leilani, laugh. Perfect timing.

"Sorry, little one!" Tio yelled back. "Dad? Can I?"

"Kiddo, get your ass in here and stop yelling, for fuck's sake. You're welcome in here anytime you want. You know that," I said.

Niya's eyes went wide as she stared at me and whispered, "You said a lot of bad words."

I snorted, and Seb leaned toward her, saying, "He does that a lot."

I almost flipped him off, but stopped myself before I did. It was going to be weird having younger kids in the house again.

Niya nodded at Seb, then shrugged. "Okay."

Seb and I exchanged a look, but Remi let out a little cry that had Seb up and moving to make sure the baby was okay—he was, he just needed a diaper change. For someone who had never changed a diaper before, Seb was picking up on it quickly.

Standing up, I kissed the top of Niya's head, then kissed the top of Leilani's—she was more hesitant with affection, but I wanted her to know how much I cared about her, so I kept doing that. She seemed like she liked it, she simply wasn't used to it.

I headed into the kitchen where Tio was, and after giving him a quick hug—he was moving around too much for anything more—I asked, "What else needs to come in?"

"Oh, I got it all already." He pointed at the piles and piles of trays filled with food. He'd obviously used his magic to carry it all inside.

"Do you need help?"

He shook his head. "Jorah and Basil are coming to help me."

My eyebrows lifted. "Basil is?"

Tio nodded like it wasn't a big deal. "Yep. I think he's secretly excited about the new kids."

"Yeah?"

He nodded before putting something in our huge oven. "Clover's coming with drinks in a little bit." Apparently he was already over the Basil thing. Bas was a good kid, most of the time, just a bit of a trou-blemaker when he was younger, although since his stay in Faela—the land of the fae—he seemed to have calmed down some. Actually, he'd matured quite a lot.

The back door opened, and I heard Jorah and Basil arguing over something before they greeted Seb and the kids in the living room, then came into the kitchen. Jorah gave me a hug, so I embraced him and kissed his temple. When he pulled me away, Basil wrinkled his nose like he was afraid I was about to force a hug on him. Which… okay, I forced a hug on him. Whatever, he needed one, and so did I.

When I kissed Bas's temple, he groaned, pushed me off him, and wiped it off. "Gross, Ailin."

I smirked. He was one of the only kids that still called me Ailin; most of the others called me *Dad* now. To be fair, Basil was my biolog-ical younger brother, so I guess it was a little strange for him that I was also his adopted father.

Waving him off, I turned to Tio. "Do you need me to do anything?"

"Nope. I have more than enough help," Tio said.

Jorah snickered. "That's code for, get the hell out of my kitchen." I chuckled and walked out, hearing Jorah add, "You don't even want the two of us in here, do you?"

I didn't hear Tio's reply because I suddenly found myself with an armful of baby and my viramore saying, "He spit up everywhere. I need to go get stuff to clean it up. Hold him. And, um, maybe change his clothes."

Seb—who had spit-up all over his shirt—ran off without waiting for a response, so I turned Remi in my arms and asked him, "Did you spit up all over your Papa?" I was trying to get in the habit of calling Seb Papa in front of Remi and the girls, and Seb was saying Dad or Daddy for me. We weren't forcing the girls to call us that, obviously— that would be up to them if and when they were comfortable with it— but we didn't want to confuse Remi.

I pursed my lips and made some goofy faces at Remi as I walked into the living room and straight to the changing table. We had some spare outfits there, so I got to work on cleaning him up while making goofy sounds and making Remi giggle.

Once he was all set, Seb was back in the living room with us wearing a new shirt. I asked the girls, "Do you want to go outside?" Since everyone was coming, we decided to hang out in the yard so we had more space. Tio was cooking something on the grill too—but no meat since all of us witches were vegetarians.

"Sure," Leilani said.

"Yes!" Niya yelled. That kid was loud and crazy, just like half the Ellwoods. It made me chuckle.

Niya ran ahead, so I walked behind Seb, who was staying with Leilani. He leaned in toward her and quietly asked, "Are you still okay with this? You don't have to stay down here if you don't want to."

"I'm okay." She sent him a hesitant smile, but it reached her eyes.

Seb gave her a nod. "Good."

Seb was able to handle things more delicately than me, for the most part, so it didn't surprise me that those two were getting along so well. Seb sharing that he'd grown up in the orphanage seemed to resonate with Leilani, so I was glad they had that connection now.

Remi pulled my hair. "Ow, fuck." I winced as I untangled my hair from his tiny fingers that were deceptively strong.

"Need me to pull your hair up or something?" Seb called without even glancing my way.

"No," I called back.

Remi grabbed a new chunk of my hair and started chewing on it.

"That's so gross, Dad," Clover said as she walked up to the house with a giant floating bubble of a bunch of drinks. "You shouldn't let him do that."

I huffed. "I'm not fucking doing it on purpose."

She rolled her eyes and took her magical bubble over to the coolers.

Seb and Leilani laid out a blanket I didn't know Seb had grabbed, then Seb put a few baby toys on it, so I set Remi down on his back, and he immediately rolled onto his stomach and did a cute inch worm type of thing toward a rattle. He grabbed it and put it in his mouth.

"He is definitely a mouther," I muttered.

"Huh?" Seb tore his gaze from Remi to me.

"We're going to have to be careful since he puts everything in his mouth."

"Isn't that normal?" he asked, staring at the baby again.

I shrugged. "Yeah, but some kids do it more than others. He does it a lot."

Seb nodded, but got distracted by his Bonded dragon zooming out of the trees and crash landing into Seb's chest. Zammerra started chattering like she was telling him a long story about what she'd hunted in the forest. As Seb sat on the blanket beside Remi with Zamm in his lap, baby and dragon both curious of each other, my Bonded came running out of the trees. I bent over to catch Seraphina in her housecat form, then I carried her to the other side of Remi and sat down. Naturally, Sera hopped off my lap and jumped onto Seb's so she could snuggle with Zamm.

I sighed and shook my head, then stretched out.

Remi kept poking the dragon and cat, but after both Bonded gave him a few licks on his face, they ignored him and decided taking a nap would be better than entertaining the baby. I shook my head at them, then watched Niya and Leilani. Leilani had been pulled into a lounge chair beside Clover, who was talking her ear off. And Niya was running around the yard, kicking a ball around with Thayer—another of my sons—and his viramore Toby.

As more and more of our family arrived, and they all welcomed Leilani, Niya, and Remi with open arms into our family, I relaxed and couldn't help but bask in the peace of the moment.

When we'd been fighting in the Berserker War, days like this had seemed like a wild fantasy, but this right here was exactly what we'd fought so hard for. Love and family. It was a perfect day.

THE DAYS TURNED INTO WEEKS, AND I TREASURED THE TIME SEB AND I had with the kids, but I knew we were going to have to go back to work soon. We'd both taken off for two months—a luxury we were allowed after helping save the world a few times—but that time was coming to an end soon.

He and I were sitting on the back deck, Remi in my lap letting me bounce him and sing him silly songs, Leilani with her earbuds in and drawing in her sketchpad, and Niya running around with my niece Esadora, who was only a year older than Niya.

Niya and Esadora stopped running and were staring at something on the ground for a few seconds before Niya knelt down, scooped whatever it was up, then ran across the yard to us. Esadora lost interest and went to see what Leilani was drawing.

Seb was playing peek-a-boo with Remi, so he didn't realize Niya was standing beside his chair until she yelled, "Look what we found!"

Seb turned, and his smiling face went from happy to complete terror so fast I wished I'd recorded him. He yelled out and jumped over the back of the chair—I didn't know he was capable of jumping that high—and ran behind me, yelling, "Get it, Ailin!"

A laugh bubbled out of me, and surprisingly, Niya giggled instead of getting scared herself. The baby, however, reacted to Seb's terror by crying, and Leilani was staring at Seb with wide eyes before she started chuckling too with Esadora laughing beside her.

"Ailin! Get it!" Seb yelled.

Niya thrust her arms forward, toward my viramore, making him scream again, as she said, "It's just a frog."

"Oh god," Seb yelled with a shudder. Remi screamed again, and Seb reached over me, grabbed the baby, pulled him to his chest, and said to him, "Don't worry, I'll protect you."

I stood and shook my head. "I see how it is, detective. You throw me to the wolves anytime there's a cute little animal or a bug, but you protect him, huh?"

"Yes. Every time," he said without hesitation and gave my shoulder a tiny nudge toward the frog.

I chuckled. "Ass."

"Get it out of here, A." He started backing away, and the look of glee on Niya's face made me laugh harder. The frog seemed content to stay in her hands—she was a half-nymph after all and clearly knew how to hold him properly.

Instead of taking the frog from her, I said, "Wanna see how fast he can run?"

She giggled. "Yes!"

"Don't you dare, Ailin Ellwood!" Seb yelled, already running off the porch while cradling Remi, who was laughing again at the movement.

"Go get him," I said to Niya.

She giggled and ran after him.

Seb took off like a shot through the yard with Niya cracking up laughing.

Leilani said, "That was so mean," but she was grinning and trying not to laugh herself.

You are dead, Ailin! Seb shouted in my head. *Dead! You're sleeping on the couch tonight!*

That only made me laugh harder, but I did hop off the porch and call out, "Okay, okay. Ni, can you bring me the frog?"

Seb ran behind me and back up on the porch, glaring the whole way. Niya came over, smiling widely as she handed me the frog and said, "He's a good frog. We should take him to the lake."

The Ellwood property had a huge lake on it, down a long path. "That's a good idea. Do you want to walk with me?"

"Sure!"

"You coming, Esadora?" I called over to her.

"Okay," she said, running off the porch to catch up.

"Dead, Ailin Talamh Ellwood!" Seb yelled.

I chuckled, but I knew I'd have some major sucking up to do later.

"Come on, baby," I said as I climbed on top of him on the bed.

"Ailin." Seb sighed and tried to push me off, but I didn't budge.

"Sebastian."

He sighed again and put his hands behind his head, staring at our bedroom ceiling. The kids were all in bed, so I started my groveling the second we came in here. The door was open—we were still keeping it that way for the time being—so I had to keep my voice down. I started kissing his neck and nibbling on his vitmea mark. He shivered, but sighed, so I leaned up to make eye contact.

"Are you really mad?"

He shook his head. "No. Don't be dumb."

"Then what's wrong?"

"Nothing."

"Seb, you keep sighing."

He hesitated, but eventually sighed again. "The door's open. I'm not letting you get me all worked up with the door open."

I grinned at that and waved my hand toward the door, calling on my nature magic—specifically on the wind—to gently close the door. "All fixed. We'll open it back up after we finish."

Leaning up, I claimed his lips, and he wrapped his arms around me, then hauled me farther on top of his body, making me moan against him. "I'm sorry I was mean to you."

He sighed. "For fuck's sake, A, it's fine."

I kissed along his jaw and down his neck, pulling the collar of his shirt down to give me better access. His hands slipped under my t-shirt where he began running his fingertips up and down my back. "This whole wearing clothes to bed thing is annoying."

He snorted. "It's not like we were sleeping naked all the time before."

"No, but you at least slept shirtless."

"Only because you're always plastered to my chest and you're like a furnace in the night. I just used you as a blanket."

I chuckled and began lifting his shirt, but a loud cry came through the monitor. I sighed and rested my forehead on Seb's chest.

"That is all you," he said over the crying.

"Technically, it's your turn."

"Technically, you scared the shit out of me earlier. You're lucky I didn't piss myself."

I snorted. "I love when you talk sexy to me."

He nudged me with a chuckle. "Shut up. Go get the baby."

"But you'll be asleep by the time I get back."

"Yep." He popped the P.

I sighed and leaned up to kiss his lips before rolling out of the bed. "I'm going to ask Opal to watch the kids tomorrow."

"Are you seriously going to ask your sister to babysit so we can have sex?"

"Yes."

"We did it in the shower when she stopped by. It was embarrassing enough knowing she knew."

"You'll have to learn to live with it." I heard him sigh as I slipped out of the room before he could argue with me and rushed into Remi's room. He was all red and had tears all over his face. My poor little squirt. "Shh, Daddy's here," I whispered as I lifted him into my arms. "I've got you, baby boy." I started rocking him as I flipped on the light and went over to the changing table. Once he was in a fresh diaper, I moved to the rocking chair, placed him on my chest and started rocking as I sang a lullaby to him.

He fussed for a little while, and his little fists held tight to my shirt like he was afraid I was going to disappear on him. I hugged him to me as I continued rocking him and promised him I would always be there for him.

CHAPTER FIVE

SEBASTIAN

When I woke, Ailin wasn't in the bed, which was weird since the sun wasn't even up yet and the kids should still be asleep. Reaching out with our viramore link, I sighed in relief that he was safe, unharmed, and asleep. And I knew exactly where I'd find him.

Rubbing the sleep out of my eyes, I padded across the hall to Remi's room, and couldn't help but smile at Ailin asleep in the rocking chair with Remi sleeping on his chest. It wasn't the first time it happened and probably wouldn't be the last.

As sweet as it was, I didn't want him to have a crick in his neck all day tomorrow, so I walked over and brushed the hair out of his face, whispering, "Ailin."

He started to blink awake.

"Hey, sweetheart, you fell asleep in the rocking chair again."

He made a face as he stretched his neck, and I frowned because he must've been here for a while already if he was sore.

"Come back to bed."

He yawned and stretched his legs out without moving Remi around too much, then whispered in a hoarse voice, "I don't want to put him down."

I kissed Ailin's forehead. "Then bring him with you."

He nodded and gently stood. Remi stirred as Ailin shifted him in his arms, but he didn't wake up. Silently, we walked across the hall, and I helped him climb into the bed with the baby. He lay on his back with Remi still on his chest.

"Do you want me to move him?" I asked.

He shook his head. "He's holding onto my shirt."

When I looked closer, I saw Remi's little fists curled around Ailin's t-shirt. It was sweet. "How are you going to sleep like that?"

Ailin shrugged. "When Jorah was little, he used to sleep on me like this. I used a spell to keep me from rolling and hurting him and to keep him from falling off."

That made me smile. "Okay. Go back to sleep. Niya will be up soon."

"Aren't you coming back to bed?"

I shook my head. "No, I'm gonna go start breakfast."

He frowned at me, so I leaned over and kissed his lips, then kissed the top of Remi's head and left them to it despite knowing Ailin wanted me to stay. I'd gotten more sleep last night than the previous three combined, so I felt pretty damn rested.

When I walked into the kitchen, I jumped and gasped out, "Holy shit!" I hadn't expected anyone to be in there this early, so seeing a person fiddling with the coffee pot scared the shit out of me.

Are you okay? What's wrong? Ailin's panicked voice startled me further.

I'm fine. Jorah's in the kitchen. Scared the crap out of me.

Scared me, too.

Sorry.

It's fine. His amusement was clear in his voice.

Jorah turned around with a smile. "Sorry. Didn't mean to scare you. Did I wake you up?"

I shook my head. "No, but, Jesus, you scared the hell out of me."

He chuckled and turned back to the counter. "Coffee?"

"Yes, please." I walked farther into the kitchen and opened the fridge to figure out what to make for breakfast. "Not that I don't want you here, but why are you here so early?"

He sighed. "I couldn't sleep and I figured you guys would be up early with Remi." He shrugged, trying to look casual, but he didn't hit the mark.

"What's wrong?" When he shook his head, I closed the fridge, leaned my hip against the counter to face him, and said, "You know you can talk to me, Jor."

He ran a hand through his hair and mirrored my position. "I've been having nightmares."

When he didn't elaborate, I asked, "Do you want to talk about it?"

"I don't know, maybe." He shrugged and turned away from me.

I grabbed his arm and pulled him over to the kitchen island where some stools were. "Come on. Talk to me."

He sighed again, and I waited patiently while he gathered his thoughts. Finally, he said, "I have nightmares sometimes about that day on the field, you know, when… when Thay, Bas, and I took on the Three magic?"

I cringed. I had nightmares from the war, too, but at least I'd been an adult when I'd seen all those horrors. I nodded.

"The magic was painful, you know?"

I didn't know personally, but considering his skin had started cracking like he was made of porcelain from the power of that magic, yeah, I could imagine.

"And it was dark magic before we were taken to Faela. It felt slimy and dirty and evil. It felt like… like I could feel all the millions of souls it had killed over the course of a thousand years. I don't know if it's memories of those souls or just things my mind conjures up, but sometimes I think I'm dreaming about them… the people the magic killed while it was under the control of evil beings."

I had no idea what to even say to that, so I rubbed Jorah's back, hoping to find the right words. After a few minutes, I said, "They say that sometimes it's good to talk to someone about these things."

"I'm talking to you."

"You know what I mean. And I'm absolutely always here whenever you want to talk about them."

He offered me a small smile. "I know. Thank you."

I nodded, and he leaned into my hand on his back a little, so I kept it there.

After several minutes, he said, "There's these other dreams that feel different, more urgent, I guess. Or maybe not urgent, but more like they're things that are happening now instead of things that already happened, if that makes sense. Someone's in hiding with their family, but the images are never clear, it's just the feelings I get from them. I have those dreams more when I'm in Faela... I don't know, I'm not doing a good job explaining them."

I squeezed his shoulder, then went back to rubbing his back. "That's okay. I think I understand what you mean. Is the Three magic clairvoyant?"

He pursed his lips, thinking for a minute. "Not particularly, no, but I suppose it could be."

I nodded. "So maybe you're picking up on things from other people."

"Maybe, but then why isn't anything clear? If I'm meant to help someone, why can't I see anything?"

"You said they're in hiding, right?" He nodded. "Maybe there's some kind of magic that's protecting them from being found, even by you."

He sighed and nodded.

"If they're that good at hiding, it stands to reason that whoever they're hiding from can't find them either."

He offered me a small smile. "That's true, I guess."

I squeezed his shoulder again, then his neck. "I'm sorry you're having nightmares about the war. Your dad and I both have them sometime, too."

"You do?"

I nodded. "We have them occasionally now, but right after the war, neither of us could sleep well."

"Even Ailin?"

I hesitated, then sighed and nodded. "He used to wake up screaming... sometimes he was screaming for you, Thayer, and Basil."

Jorah winced. "I'm sorry."

"It's not your fault, bud, not even a little bit."

That made him smile sadly. "It *is* a little bit my fault. I'm the one that found the right spell and rushed out into a fucking battle, grabbed my brothers, and pulled that magic into us. Definitely my fault a little."

I huffed. "No, Jor, it's not. You couldn't have predicted what was going to happen any more than the rest of us. None of that's your fault, bud."

He shrugged. "I feel like I made everyone suffer while we were gone, though."

"Like I said, you didn't know what was going to happen. You did the right thing."

"You really believe that?"

"Yes," I said without hesitation. "And you know that Ailin feels the same way, right? He hates what happened, he hates that you had to bear that burden, but he knows you did the right thing and he's proud of you for it. Your dad's always been so proud of you because you're an amazing kid, we both have been. You did what you thought was right, you saved us, you saved everyone in this entire realm from that magic. You're a hero, Jorah Brenainn Ellwood. Don't you ever doubt that."

He took a shaky breath, then leaned over to hug me. I returned the embrace easily and held him tight. We hugged for a long time, and when he finally pulled away, I said, "I'm glad you came here today. You can help me make breakfast."

He chuckled at that, then sobered and admitted, "I wanted to be closer to you and Dad."

I couldn't help but pull him back into my arms for a minute. Even at eighteen, he still needed his parents sometimes. I whispered, "You are always welcome here, Jorah. Anytime at all. You can even stay in one of the rooms upstairs if you want to."

"I know, Seb. Thank you." When we parted, he wiped his eyes and asked, "What do you have in mind for breakfast?"

I squeezed his shoulder before getting up. "I have no idea."

We walked into the kitchen, and Jorah opened the fridge just as a quiet voice said, "Good morning."

I swung around to find Leilani in the doorway, one hand rubbing the other forearm, kind of shrunken into herself, trying to appear small. I hated when she felt so uncomfortable she made herself seem smaller, but it had been at least two weeks since I'd seen her do it. It made me wonder if it was because Jorah was here or if she maybe overheard us talking.

"Hey, munchkin. Did you sleep okay?" I asked.

She nodded and offered me a smile that didn't reach her eyes.

Jorah shut the fridge door, walked over to Leilani, and put his arm over her shoulders, tugging her into the kitchen as he said, "What's up, little sis?"

Part of her relaxed a little, and I couldn't help but smile. Most of the older boys had started calling her "little sis" which was sweet and hopefully helped her feel welcomed and like a part of the family.

She stared up at him and mumbled, "Hey."

I said, "We're about to make some breakfast, would you like to help?"

She smiled at me, and it reached her eyes this time. "Sure."

"Come on, then."

Jorah sent me a grin as Leilani joined me and we all finally got to making breakfast for everyone.

THE GIRLS WERE PLAYING OUTSIDE, AND REMI WAS IN HIS BOUNCER IN the corner, so Ailin and I were straightening up before dinner.

"Why are there no burp cloths left?" Ailin asked as he searched every inch of the living room like one might magically appear out of thin air.

I glared at him. "Do you remember when I asked you to flip the laundry yesterday?"

He sighed and pinched the bridge of his nose. "Motherfucker."

"Yeah, A, you fucking forgot to put the load in the dryer, so now we're out of burp cloths! And out of bibs! Bibs, A. You know how messy he gets when he's shoving food in his face." I didn't mean to yell, but it had been a frustrating day because apparently it was No-One-Listens-To-Papa-Day, and I was about to lose it. Or maybe I already had.

Ailin cringed. "I forgot."

I threw my arms up in frustration. "Of course you did. You haven't done it the last two times I asked, so why would I expect anything different this time?"

"I'm sorry."

"That does me a hell of a lot of good right now, doesn't it? You haven't been helping me at all." I stormed into the kitchen and may have started slamming cabinet doors as I got myself a glass of water… I should've just grabbed the wine, but it was a little early for that.

"I said I'm sorry!" he yelled.

"Good for you, asshole!"

"I'm pretending you said 'it's okay, asshole' instead."

I rolled my eyes and flipped him off, not that he could see me.

"I know you're flipping me off."

"Good!"

He sighed and—wisely—left me alone to go grab Remi and take him outside.

As we got ready for bed, Ailin said, "I think we need to do another family volunteer trip. Make the kids go help out somewhere like we used to right after the war. There's still so much to rebuild and clean up, but there's still so many kids in need. Ours need to remember how lucky they are, you know? Maybe give a little back."

"That's not a bad idea. It's been a while since we did anything like that all together," I agreed.

"I think we need to send them back to Eastbrook. I think it's important for the family."

"I agree." I sent him a smile before I climbed into bed with him. Once we were settled, I said, "Ailin?"

"Hm?"

"I know I was stressed today and kinda mean, but I hope you know I don't regret a thing, and… I'm sorry I yelled at you. If there's anyone I want to do this with, it's you."

He pulled me into him so my head was on his chest, as if we switched places with how we usually slept. "I know, baby. It's alright. And I'm really sorry about the laundry. I promise I won't forget next time."

"Mhm, we'll see about that."

He kissed my cheek. "I won't."

I took a breath. "Okay." After a beat, I asked, "You're not mad?"

He chuckled and squeezed me to him. "You're allowed to be pissed off at me, and you're allowed to yell. It's fine."

I chewed on my lips for a few seconds, tracing the top of one of his tattoos that was sticking out of his collar. "Still, I'm sorry."

He kissed my forehead. "It's alright, detective. Are you sure you're not mad at me anymore?"

"Nah, I'm fine. Next time, I'll just zap your ass or something, though."

He chuckled and I felt a surge of love come through our link, and I sighed in relief. There wasn't even an ounce of anger there, so I knew he meant it.

I hugged him to me as I sagged in relief and contentment, and I whispered, "I love you."

"I love you, too, baby."

❧

"Are you sure it's okay?" Ailin asked for the millionth time.

I rolled my eyes. "Yes. Go before you're late."

He sighed, planted a kiss on my lips, then one on Remi's cheek since he was in my arms—Ailin had already said goodbye to the girls —and he headed out the door.

Petunia Crane, the leader of Brinnswick, called to request Ailin's presence at a meeting concerning the funding for displaced children after the war, and even though Ailin wasn't really involved in anything "officially," it was still important for him to go. That funding was needed. Hell, they needed way more than what was given to them, so it was concerning that Ailin had been called in for this. Petunia was more of a friend than the Queen Bee to us, so we knew she'd only ask him if it was important, which was honestly, worrisome.

So here I was with the kids. *Alone* with the kids for the first time ever.

But it would be fine. Absolutely, totally fine.

IT WAS NOT FINE.

Remi had been crying for the last three hours straight. Before that, he'd napped for less than an hour, and before his nap, he'd cried for two hours straight. And nothing I did made him stop. He was absolutely miserable, and I couldn't figure out what the hell was wrong with him.

I was beginning to panic.

What if he was sick? What if something was going on and I needed to take him to the hospital?

He didn't have a fever, no sign of a rash, and he drank his bottle earlier and had peed and pooped in his diaper more than once today. Everything seemed to be in working order, but that didn't mean there wasn't something else wrong with him. I'd tried putting him on the floor to see if maybe he wanted to explore on his own some, but every time I tried, he just crawled right over to me and pulled on my legs until I picked him back up. He'd been spitting up more than usual and pooping more often, but I didn't know why. Was he upset that Ailin wasn't here with us? Could that be it? Separation anxiety, maybe? Maybe that was why he wanted to be held; he didn't want me disappearing, too.

When I used my magic to examine him, looking for injuries or illness, I couldn't find anything, but I wasn't the absolute best at that so I could've missed something.

To top it off, Leilani had been ignoring me all day. I didn't know why or what was going on with her, but yesterday, she'd been helpful and kind, and today she was acting like a moody teenager. That didn't actually happen overnight, did it? Did kids go from a sweet, innocent, kind child to a prickly, mean, moody teen in one night? Was that really a thing?

And Niya, she, well, she wasn't really doing anything differently, to be honest. She was running around the house, screaming and playing, which wasn't anything new. Except because Remi was crying so loudly, Niya had decided that she needed to be even louder than him, so… it was like the loudest house in history happening right now. I was surprised one of the older kids hadn't come by to see why there was so much screaming going on, because surely, they could hear all of this even being through the woods and half a mile away, right?

My nerves had never, ever, ever been this frazzled before. I'd been in the middle of a war and been less crazed than this. My eyes kept watering because I didn't know how to help Remi, and it was so damn loud in here that I couldn't think straight at all.

When the smell of something awful hit my nose, I wanted to gag but held it together. With a screaming baby in my arms, I went over to the changing table and remembered that I needed to open a new pack of diapers. Remi started wailing even louder, so I tried bouncing him a little, but his arms were flailing, and I couldn't get a good grip on the damn diaper pack. I was afraid I'd drop him, and I knew from experience that lying him down, even for a split-second, resulted in him screaming even louder.

I turned to the eleven-year-old that had been sitting on the couch drawing with her earbuds in all day, and said, "Leilani, please help me open these." Okay, I yelled it because it was so loud.

She looked up from her sketchpad, saw what I wanted, and immediately, looked back down at the page. Completely ignoring me. Like a bratty teenager.

I clenched my jaw, about to lose it, but then Niya leapt over the couch, her blanket tied like a cape billowing behind her, and I had a mini-heart attack, thinking she was going to break her leg. She landed, did a weird little roll, then got up and began screaming about superheroes again.

Remi let out a loud wail, and I bounced him, saying, "I know, buddy, I'm trying. I'll get you changed in a seco—"

He puked right in my face. Thank god it ended up mostly on my cheek and not in my mouth since I'd been talking to him. Holy shit-balls! What was happening right now?

I grabbed a burp cloth to wipe it off my face and his chin, then pulled out a million wipes to clean us off again. Thank god I didn't gag easily because that was horrible.

Suddenly, I felt Ailin's presence pass through our property's wards, and I didn't think I'd ever been more relieved to know he was almost home.

"Daddy's coming home!" I yelled over the noise.

Remi burped in my face.

"For fuck's sake," I muttered, trying not to breathe in that smell.

"You said a bad word!" Niya screamed at the top of her lungs.

"How the hell did you hear that, but you didn't hear me screaming at you to stop trying to dive off the table?"

She ignored me of course.

How did that little girl have so much energy all the time?

Ailin walked into the door and came around the corner, and relief flooded me. I marched over to him, thrust the baby into his arms, and said, "Never leave me alone with them again."

He put Remi over his shoulder and started patting his back, staring at me with wide eyes.

I backed away with my hands up so he couldn't hand Remi back. I just needed a minute to myself. "He pooped." I walked over to the changing table and opened up the new package of diapers, saying over my shoulder to Leilani, "Was it really that difficult to help open these?" I ran past Ailin, yelling over the screaming, "Good luck with that. I'm taking a shower... where I can cry in peace." I only murmured the last part, but I thought he heard me through our link. I grimaced in Ailin's direction, feeling a little bad for bailing but not bad enough to stop, then I disappeared up the stairs.

A few seconds later, I heard Ailin yell, "Ow! Why would you do that?" I could only assume that Superhero Niya had attacked.

As I rushed to our bedroom and into the attached bathroom, I jumped in the shower since I hadn't been able to shower yet today. The water was heavenly, and the best part was that the screaming downstairs was far enough away and drowned out by the noise of the water that I could ignore it.

Not even two minutes later, Ailin asked through our link, *Seb, when are you coming back down?*

Never, I replied.

Sebastian. Come on.

I swear to god, Ailin. I've had them all day, you can deal with them for twenty minutes while I take a shower and get the baby's poop out of my hair!

He didn't reply immediately. *How did you get poop in your hair?*

You don't want to know.

I washed my hair out, then started shampooing it again. It was going to need a few extra washes.

After my third rinse, Ailin said, *Sebastian?*

What?

I love you.

I love you, too.

You know you're gorgeous, right? And amazing.

That made me pause, and I shook my head while rolling my eyes even though he couldn't see me. *Being nice to me isn't going to get me to come back down there any faster.*

Worth a try. He sounded slightly amused.

Don't worry, only two hours until bedtime, I told him.

Holy fuck.

Tell me about it.

Ailin let me be after that, but I didn't take very long because I was still worried about Remi, and to be honest, about Leilani as well. She wasn't acting like herself today.

When I walked downstairs, Remi was still screaming, Leilani still on the couch, and Niya was now sitting at the table coloring… but she was singing at the top of her lungs, so it wasn't any quieter.

Ailin shot me a strained grin as I walked into the living room, and he said, "I think I've had to clean myself up at least three times since I've been home."

I nodded. "That spell gets old after a while. Do you need to take a shower?"

"No, I'm clean now, so it's all good." He was practically yelling to be heard over Remi.

"Any idea about what's wrong with him?"

"Aspen thinks he could be teething," he said. I wasn't surprised he'd called his sister since she had kids of her own and might know what to do. I'd thought the same.

I sighed. "That's the same thing she told me earlier."

"You called her?"

"He's been crying all day, so yeah, I called this morning."

He nodded and bounced the little boy. "Nothing appears to be wrong with him."

"I know, but he's clearly uncomfortable. He doesn't usually throw up this much."

"That could be from all the crying."

I lifted a shoulder. "True. So what do we do?"

"I don't know, Seb."

Hearing our little boy sounding like he was in pain was killing me, so I reached over and pulled him out of Ailin's arms so I could hug him. His crying quieted down for a few seconds before he went back to wailing.

"We're definitely having leftovers tonight."

I nodded in agreement, then said through our link, *Do you think we should find out what's bothering Leilani? She's been like that all day, and not that I want her to feel like she has to help all the time, but she usually does. She's barely said two words to me all day, and even ignored me when I asked her to pass me the burp cloth that was literally right next to her. Something's going on with her, but I haven't been able to talk to her over all the screaming all day.*

I'll talk to her.

Thanks. I'll take Remi in the other room so you can hear her. Maybe he'll chew on one of the chewy things we have in the freezer for him.

Ailin nodded and kissed my cheek before I walked out of the room, carrying a screaming infant and heading for a loudly singing four-year-old.

CHAPTER SIX

AILIN

As I sat down beside Leilani, I pulled her earbuds out and angled myself on the couch to face her. "What's going on with you?"

She crossed her arms over her chest and tilted her face away from me.

"Leilani, I need you to talk to me. I can't help you if I don't know what's wrong." When she still didn't say anything, I sighed and leaned back on the couch, resting my hands on my stomach and trying to seem relaxed even though I was anything but. "Why wouldn't you help Seb out when I was working? You know this was the first time he's been left alone with a baby, right? He was already nervous, and today turned into a clusterfuck."

She shrugged.

"Come on, Lani, please talk to me, kiddo. You've always seemed like you enjoyed helping with Remi. What happened today?"

She huffed and continued staring off, so I decided to wait her out. We sat in silence—well, we were quiet, Remi and Niya were loud as fuck—for what felt like an eternity, but eventually, she said, "If you're sending us back, just get on with it."

I sat up straight and grabbed her arm. "Why in the hell would you say something like that?"

She moved her arm out of my grasp and turned away. "You and Seb don't want to keep us."

"Leilani, I promise you that we do. We both love you, and we're happy to have you as part of our family." They'd been with us for nearly two months, why would she suddenly think we didn't want them?

She peeked over her shoulder at me and asked in a defeated voice, "Then why were you talking about sending us back there?"

"What are you talking about? Who said that?"

"Last night, I heard you and Seb talking about sending us back."

My brow furrowed as I tried to remember what in the world she was talking about. "We never said that, Lani."

She narrowed her eyes at me. "You said that you wanted to send us back to Eastbrook and that it would be better for the whole family."

I blinked at her, not understanding at first, and then I closed my eyes in frustration as I realized what she'd heard. "Kiddo, you must've only heard part of the conversation. We were talking about sending our older kids over there to help volunteer because it's been a while since any of them have. I was going to make them go back... to help out."

"What?"

"We used to take our kids to volunteer with cleaning up Brinnswick after the war, and I took a few of them to Eastbrook to help paint and shit. It's been a long time since I've taken any of them with me because they're all so busy now. I thought that since we'd adopted you guys, it would be nice to do some volunteer work there since we can't bring home any more kids." I shrugged. "I thought it would be a good thing to help out where we can."

She slowly turned to me, and seeing the tears in her eyes broke my heart. "Y-you mean it? That's really what you meant?"

I gently placed my hand on her back. "I promise you. There is no part of me, or of Seb, that wants to send you back."

Her face fell. "Even after today? I ignored him while you were at work. I was mean."

"Even after today," I agreed. "There is nothing you could do that will ever make you not a part of our family. You're an Ellwood now, kiddo. And trust me, you've got nothing on the shit Basil and Thayer used to pull around here."

She snorted and wiped her nose. "I'm sorry I didn't help out." Her gaze moved to the hands in her lap. "I just… I was coming to see if I could get a glass of water, I heard you say that, and I thought… when I heard it, I decided I wanted you to send us back sooner rather than to keep getting Niya's hopes up that this was our new family, so I thought if I… if I wasn't nice, then maybe you'd send us back before Niya ended up with a broken heart." It was clear she meant both of them winding up with broken hearts. This poor kid.

Wrapping my arm over her shoulders, I pulled her to my side and kissed her temple. "Nothing you do will ever make us send you back. This is your home, we are your family, whether you like it or not, you're stuck with us for the rest of your life."

"You really mean that?" she asked in a small voice.

"Yes," Sebastian said as he walked into the living room—he'd put Remi in his swing that he'd pushed into the dining room—and sat on the coffee table in front of Leilani. He wrapped his hands around her tiny ones and squeezed. "I'm sorry if I ever made you question your place here, munchkin. This is your home, your family, and we love you so much. You really are stuck with us forever now. I promise that will never, ever, ever change, Lani. No matter what, we're your family."

She let out a watery laugh before throwing her tiny arms around Seb's neck in a tight hug that he returned. After waiting a few seconds, I put my arms around both of them and held on tight as Leilani cried and apologized a million times for ignoring Seb all day long.

They finally separated when the baby's cries went up a few dozen notches. Seb opened his mouth, but I stood, saying, "I'll get him." I kissed both their heads on the way out of the living room. Following the horrendous stench, I found myself in the middle of a horrible, terrible stink bomb.

"My Mother, kiddo, what in the hell did you eat?" I asked Remi as I headed into the warzone.

Remi stopped wailing so loud—although he was still crying—when he saw me. I hurriedly cleaned him up and got rid of the dirty diaper, then started gently rocking him. He was so agitated and I was wondering if he had an upset belly, although I didn't know what could've caused it. Everything he'd eaten yesterday had been the usual things, and we hadn't switched his formula or anything.

"He's stinky today," Niya said from her spot at the dining table where she was still coloring.

"I know, sweetie pie."

"And loud. Louder than me."

I snorted and patted her on the head. "I don't know how that's possible."

She giggled and stuck her tongue out, then suddenly covered her picture with her whole body. "Don't look!"

"Are you making me something?"

She nodded.

"Okay, I won't look, pumpkin." I'd adopted Seb's nickname for her. "I'm going to walk Remi around for a minute, are you okay if I go outside?"

She nodded again.

"You can come out if you want. We'll have dinner soon."

She shook her head. "I wanna finish."

"Alright, kiddo." I kissed the top of her head as I walked past her and focused on Remi. "Hey, baby boy, what's going on with you?" I whispered as I peeked into the living room. Seb and Leilani were talking quietly, but Lani was actually smiling, so I'd take it.

Knowing it was a nice evening out, I carried Remi out back and started walking around the perimeter of the house, hoping the fresh air would do him some good. He kept fussing, though.

I rubbed his back and bounced him, but nothing seemed to help. "Don't worry, kiddo, we're going to figure out what's going on with you." I kissed his little head and started singing a lullaby that my mother used to sing to me, the same one I'd sung to all my other kids after they'd been in my care. It was a sweet and silly song about love but sung in my native language—Caillea.

Remi cried through the first verse, but when I got to the chorus and began rocking him, he blinked up at me. I almost laughed at the cute face of confusion he was giving me, but I managed to keep it together and continue singing.

Since it was the only thing that seemed to be calming him, I sang the song a second time, watching as he drifted off to sleep. When I finished the song, I sighed in relief and turned to go back inside only to find my viramore standing in the doorway, leaning against the doorjamb with his arms and ankles crossed and a small smile on his face.

He said through our link, *You have a good voice.*

You only like it because it got the baby to sleep.

I felt his amusement through our link. *That's a definite bonus, but I like your voice, too. Maybe you can sing me to sleep.*

I bit on my lips to prevent me from laughing and waking Remi. *You need me to rock you, too?*

He rolled his eyes, shook his head, and headed back inside. *Come on, let's eat and do bath time, then we can get these little boogers to sleep.*

Sounds good.

It didn't go as planned. Well, Niya and Leilani went to sleep alright, but Remi woke up before I finished eating, and he'd been crying since. My poor viramore looked like he was going to pull his hair out.

"Are you okay?"

"Not really," he admitted. "He's so miserable, and I don't know how to fix it." Seb met my eyes, and after a few seconds, his honey orbs filled with tears.

"Oh, baby, come here." I opened my free arm up, and Seb slid over to me.

We were in our bed, and Remi was crying in my arms. He was crying quietly instead of the loud wailing he'd been doing earlier, but I was sure the only reason he wasn't as loud was because he'd actually lost his voice. And now Seb was crying, too.

"I'm sorry," Seb said, wiping his eyes. "I just don't know how to help him."

I pulled him in and kissed his forehead. "It's alright. We'll figure it out. He's likely only teething."

He nodded and leaned into me. "Need me to take him?"

"No, I've got him. Try to get some sleep while he's quiet."

He nodded, and we both lay down with Remi between us.

After a few seconds, Seb asked, "What was the meeting about?"

"Some of the representatives in the Brinnswick Union think they're giving too much money to the displaced children initiative."

"Are you serious? What the hell is wrong with them?"

I sighed. "I know. Emrys and Julius were there with me, backing me up, and Petunia was as well, but I don't know. Those people don't seem to realize what pulling that money could do to those kids and those programs." Having two of my coven members—Emrys and Julius—there to help had been a small blessing. Those two were often so busy with all the government things that they were hardly home with us. Even though the circumstances were awful, it had been nice to see two of our vampire coven members today. Not that I wanted to admit to Seb that, despite the horrible dumbasses trying to take away money from kids, I'd had a nice time with Jules and Em during the breaks when he'd been living in Puke and Poo Hell today. My poor viramore.

I kissed Seb's forehead again and whispered, "Go to sleep. This isn't going to be solved anytime soon, and it's nothing to worry about right now."

He blew out a breath and tiredly whispered, "Okay."

Seb was out in seconds, and luckily, Remi followed after that.

All night long, Seb and I had to take turns holding Remi so the other could get a little sleep. It was an awful night.

CHAPTER SEVEN

SEBASTIAN

"He hasn't stopped crying since yesterday, Ailin. What if something's wrong? What if he's sick? We should take him to the hospital right now," I said, bouncing Remi with my stomach in knots, my exhaustion making me sluggish and grumpy.

"He doesn't have a fever or anything, and I can't find anything wrong with him," he replied over top of Remi's crying.

The poor baby seemed like he was so uncomfortable, but Ailin was right, we couldn't find any injuries or illnesses in him. We'd both reached out with our magic to see if we could figure out what was going on with the little man. We'd even had every single one of our kids—and their viramores—that were home come and check as well. No one could figure out anything.

I kept bouncing him in my arms, but I'd have to get up off the blanket soon and walk around. We'd brought the kids outside for some fresh air to see if that would help, and to let Niya run off some energy, because wow, was that kid hyper. Leilani was playing with Niya, Sera, and Zamm, so at least they were having fun.

"Want me to take him for a little while?" Ailin asked.

Part of me wanted to hand him over, but knowing that something was wrong with Remi made me want to hold him close and never let go. "I don't know."

Ailin opened his mouth to respond, but Remi let out a loud and horrible scream.

"Oh my god, what's wrong, Remi?" I asked as I pulled him off my shoulder to examine him. A huge shiver went through his entire body, and it didn't seem completely natural. "Did you see that, A?"

"Yeah, put him on the blanket, Seb." When I didn't move, Ailin said, "Put him down, Sebastian. Now."

I shot Ailin an angry glare for being an asshole, but didn't spare any time on it because that didn't matter right now. Carefully, I placed Remi on the blanket, but hovered right over him so I could scoop him up quickly.

The weird shiver ran over his body again, and I swore it was like his skin rippled.

Ailin's whispered, "Holy shit," made my stomach clench further.

When the ripple went through a third time, I gasped at what I was seeing. "Is that…"

"Yeah, it's fur."

Before Ailin could elaborate, Remi grunted loudly and his skin suddenly grew… fur. Gray fur.

I couldn't figure out what the hell was happening to our baby, but Ailin was in motion, using his green magic to strip the baby's clothing off in only a few seconds. He even removed Remi's diaper so he was lying there naked.

"A, what the hell are you do—" I cut myself off with a grunt.

Remi's entire body began contorting and moving in unnatural ways as fur sprouted up all over him, but his cries turned into a few little whimpers. His face sort of elongated, his ears grew, his limbs changed shapes, his hands and feet turning into paws. I'd never see anything so terrifying. It felt like it lasted forever, but it was less than a minute before Remi shook himself out. Only now instead of a baby lying on the blanket, there was a little wolf pup staring up at us.

"R-Remi?" I whispered, a hand covering my mouth.

He let out a little bark.

"Holy fucking shit."

"He's a shifter," Ailin whispered. "Holy hell, Remi's not a human, he's a fucking shifter!"

I could only stare at our little boy that was now our little… wolf. What the fucking fuck?

"Remi?" Ailin said. "It's okay, kiddo, you're safe now. You're going to be okay." Ailin reached toward the baby—the pup—and right before he made contact, Remi hopped backward, out of the way.

The pup stared up at Ailin with his tongue hanging out and his tail wagging. He might've only been eight months as a human and not yet walking—though he was already pretty damn close for so young—but as an eight-month-old wolf pup, he was very capable of standing and walking.

I reached out to try and pet him.

And running. He was perfectly capable of running.

"Shit!" Ailin yelled as Remi took off across the yard. "Shit shit, motherfucking shit." Ailin stood and ran after him. "We can't let him run into the woods!"

My eyes widened at that, and I hopped to my feet.

Leilani and Niya both started screaming, and Leilani yelled, "What is that thing?"

"It's your brother!" I yelled back. "Don't hurt him!"

"That's Remi?" Niya screeched.

"Yes!" Ailin and I both yelled back.

"A, put a shield around the yard so he doesn't run out!"

Ailin stopped running and immediately pulled on his green nature magic as I ran past him, trying to catch up to the little wolf that was yelping and running like he was having the time of his life.

Luckily, Ailin managed to get the shield up with Remi still in the yard, but after chasing him for a few minutes, I stopped running and held my side since I now had a stitch. Jesus, I was out of shape. Panting, I fell to the ground and lay on my back, trying to catch my breath. Holy shit, apparently a baby wolf was hella good at running and quicker than I could've expected.

I would've used magic to catch him, but I didn't want to freak him out. This was the first time in over twenty-four hours that Remi wasn't crying.

Ailin plopped in the grass beside me, panting as much as I was, but he remained sitting up as he watched our little boy, who was apparently a fucking shifter, run circles around his sisters.

"How the hell did we miss that?" I asked. "Why didn't we know he was a shifter?"

"I've never met a shifter that young. He felt like a human."

"That's weird."

"Shifters are the result of fae having babies with humans. Sometimes it skips generations before the tiny bit of the fae genes forces a shift."

I wrinkled my nose. "Ew, do Nik and Talon have kids and grandkids here?"

"No. I asked Nik that before. Neither of them have ever had children. Nik was offended I asked since the fae that do that are looked down on, apparently. They have babies with humans and leave the child with no way of knowing the possibility of being a shifter is even a thing. It's fucking terrible, especially when most of the humans they sleep with don't even know they're fucking fae. And it's not like humans have a test to figure out whether they have fae blood or not."

I waved all that off. "Ailin, our kid is a fucking shifter. We know nothing about shifters."

He sighed. "I know. We can talk to Alec about it."

I glanced at him and shook my head. "But Alec isn't a shifter, he's a werewolf. He doesn't control his shifts, the moon does."

"But he knows what it's like to change form, which is more than either of us know."

I grunted and turned my head to watch as Remi tried jumping up to bite the hem of Niya's shirt. He was a shifter, which was good on the one hand because shifters had longer lives and better healing abilities than humans, so it meant he wasn't as vulnerable as we'd thought, but on the other hand, he turned into a fucking wolf. What the hell were we supposed to do with that? I scrubbed my hand over my face. "How do we get him to turn back?"

"No idea."

I groaned. "You're supposed to know these things, A."

He looked amused when I caught his eyes. "I have no experience with this at all."

"Maybe we can bribe him with food. He likes those little baby wheel snack thingies."

Ailin shrugged. "Worth a try."

"Ailin, this couldn't have been the first time he's shifted, right?" There was no way Remi had a *catalyst event* while in our care.

Anger crossed over Ailin's face, his eyes flashing with green smoke, and he said, "No, it isn't the first time. We can't talk about this right now."

Panic and worry clawed at me, but I knew he was right. Not only were we both going to be pissed when we talked, but we didn't want to worry Remi or the girls about it. Right now, we needed to make sure Remi was safe and that all three of the kids knew how much we loved them, whether they were covered in fur or not.

I gave Ailin a nod, then headed over to where Remi was yipping away at Niya as she giggled at him.

Leilani asked, "How come he can walk like that, but not when he's, you know, a person?"

I shrugged. "He's still a person, just in a new form. Wolf form, and his other one is his human form, I guess?" I waved that away. We could figure out the terminology later. "Anyway, I guess because an eight-month-old wolf pup can walk and a human one can't?" I had no idea if that was the case or not, but it sounded good. "Plus, he can crawl in his human form, so maybe it's similar?" Again, no clue. "We need to do a lot of research about shifters."

She nodded. "I can help you."

I smiled at her. "That would be really great, Lani."

She nodded, then knelt down and held her hand out to the baby—er, to the wolf pup. "Come here, Remi. That's a good boy. That's right, come here, little brother."

I grinned over at Ailin and said through our link, *That's the first time she's called him that.*

I know. He nodded at me with a smile, although he was really fucking tense, still upset about the situation.

He wasn't pissed that Remi was a shifter. Far from it in fact. Knowing he had a longer lifespan than a human was a blessing. Ailin was pissed about the why and how of it, and if I stopped to think about it, I was sure I would explode in anger, so I set it aside for now. Ailin and I would discuss it after the kids went to bed tonight. We had to focus on our little boy. We needed to make sure that Remi—and the girls—were comfortable in their own skin, no matter what that looked like.

So I knelt beside Leilani with my hand out and said, "You're such a pretty wolf, Remi. So sweet. I bet you're soft." I didn't know how much he could understand even in human form, but he'd be able to understand my tone. "Come here, baby boy."

Remi stretched his neck toward me, his little cute nose twitching as he sniffed. Then he suddenly rushed forward, almost knocking me on my ass. I caught him, laughing, then plopped down on the ground so I could hold him in my lap. Chuckling, I kept petting him and giving him some good scratches, and Leilani sat cross-legged right in front of me, petting him as well. Niya came over and sat to my side to join in, and Ailin sat on my other side, resting his cheek against my upper arm. My poor viramore was having trouble keeping his anger in check. We both knew something terrible had to have happened to Remi. It was bad enough when we'd known he'd been left at the orphanage with no information about him, that his biological parents had stranded him there, but now we knew that on top of that, something horrific had to have happened to him. A catalyst event. Maybe him shifting was why he'd been left at Eastbrook.

Of course I was grateful beyond measure that he'd been left there —and thank god his biological parents did at least that much—but knowing he'd come from tragedy was a hard pill to swallow.

"He's so cute," Leilani said with a grin. "I mean, he's always cute, but this is so cool. I can't believe he isn't human."

"Me either," Ailin said, his voice thick.

I leaned over to kiss his temple. I left my lips on his skin and closed my eyes for a moment, breathing him in. When I pulled back, he grabbed my hand and kissed the back of it. The kids were pretty used to our PDA by this point so they didn't notice; it wasn't like we did anything inappropriate around them.

The five of us sat there together for a long time with Remi soaking up all the attention. He had a wolfy grin on his face that was adorable.

Zammerra and Seraphina trotted over and joined our little group. They both gave Remi some sniffs, then each licked his face a few times before Zamm jumped to my shoulders and wrapped herself around my neck while Sera did the same to Ailin. Our Bonded knew we were upset, so it wasn't surprising they were offering us their own comfort.

Eventually, Remi started getting tired, so I picked him up and cradled him against my chest in the same position I'd hold him in if he was in human form. His little paws in the air were adorable. "Come on, buddy, can you shift back?"

He stared at me and nothing happened.

I exchanged a look with Ailin. "How the hell do we get him to shift back?"

Leilani cleared her throat, then hesitated before saying, "Can I try?"

"Sure," I said, then passed her the baby.

She held him the same way I did, but stood up and started rocking him and talking to him quietly, telling him how sweet and cute he was. It only took a moment for me to realize she was using her natural nymph magic—her aura—to calm him, and even though it wasn't directed at me, I could tell she was trying to put a sense of "shift to human form" into her aura. I had never felt anything like it, and in fact, I didn't even know it was possible for her to make her aura tell you what she wanted.

Ailin was still leaning into me, but now he was smiling at our daughter.

Niya climbed into my lap to watch her older sister, so I wrapped my arms around her and rested my chin on top of her head.

Ailin said in my head, *When they start school next month, we'll have to make sure there's a teacher that knows how to help them train with their magic.*

I hummed in agreement. *Can we help them at home, too?*

We can try. Talon and Nikolai will probably be able to help since they have auras like that as well.

I hid a smile at that. A few months ago, Ailin acted like Nik and Talon were the enemy. Now they were both living on our property and a part of our coven. The fact that Ailin was willing to ask for help from them was a huge step. Especially since it concerned our daughters. *That sounds good, sweetheart.*

In Leilani's arms, Remi began to wiggle and grunt, but he didn't sound like he was in pain, just frustrated, maybe. His fur rippled once, twice, then his entire body changed before our eyes. It was the weirdest thing seeing his fur flatten and change to human skin while his face slowly morphed and his paws turned to hands. He wiggled around for a few seconds after he changed back, then he tucked his little face into Leilani and promptly fell asleep. Shifting back and forth, not to mention all the running around, had probably exhausted him.

She smiled at Remi, then over at us, looking so proud and happy.

"Thank you, Lani," I said. "That was amazing."

She shrugged a little, and Ailin hopped up to help her, saying, "He's right, Lani, you were fucking amazing."

That made her laugh. "Thanks."

"Do you want me to take him so we can get a diaper on him?" Ailin asked.

She nodded, and Ailin scooped the baby into his arms, then they rushed inside.

Niya didn't move for a few minutes, which was probably the longest I'd seen her stay still for. I didn't mind one bit. I loved having her in my lap, so I didn't say a word. Eventually, she said, "I'm hungry."

"Me too. What do you want to eat?" I asked.

"Chocolate."

I snorted. "Of course you want chocolate. You always want chocolate." I tickled her belly, and she screeched in delight. "I'm gonna start calling you the chocolate monster."

"No!" She laughed and wiggled in my arms.

I stopped tickling her long enough for her to catch her breath, then I went in for more tickling. By the time I stopped, she was out of breath, but still giggling. I picked her up as I stood and carried her inside, but kept spinning around in a circle every few steps to make her laugh. Zammerra stayed on my shoulder, but was not impressed with all the spinning.

Inside, Remi was asleep in the playpen, and Leilani and Ailin were in the kitchen making some food, so Niya and I joined them.

WITH THE KIDS FINALLY IN BED, AND REMI ASLEEP AND NO LONGER uncomfortable, Ailin I shut our bedroom door so we couldn't be overheard.

"Do you think he needed to shift and couldn't figure out how?" I asked as I pet Zammerra before she settled on the pillows, curled up with Seraphina.

Ailin nodded as he began taking off his leg bracers and getting ready for bed. "That's what I think. Hopefully now that he's done it again, he'll be able to figure it out and won't get uncomfortable like that again."

"I hope so." I cringed, scratched Sera's head, and started getting ready for bed. "He's going to be able to climb out of everything now."

Ailin snorted. "Yeah, he is."

I hesitated, then puffed my cheeks and blew the air out. "Are we going to talk about it?"

He sighed.

"Ailin, we need to talk about it."

"What's there to say, Seb?"

I sighed. He always had to make things difficult. "I've researched different creatures and shit, but I don't remember every single thing, so I need to… I need to know for sure. Don't shifters not even shift until—"

"They have a catalyst event? Yeah. It's theorized that many potential shifters never turn and they remain human their entire lives because they don't have a catalyst event. The catalyst event sets something off in their DNA to force the shift."

"Which means—"

The anger he'd been holding in all day came back with a vengeance. "He had to have a traumatic experience. A catalyst event is always a terrible, horrible, and most often, a near death experience. Something terrible happened to our little boy before we adopted him. Something awful, something that he almost died from. If he wasn't a shifter, he wouldn't be here today. That's how it works. Being a shifter saves their lives, and sometimes that doesn't even save them. He's lucky he had fae in his blood or he wouldn't have been able to transform and…"

I stepped closer to my viramore. "Ailin."

He slammed his arm bracer down on the dresser. "He could've been killed before we ever met him, and there's nothing we can do about it! There's no way to find out what happened to him or who the fuck hurt him. There's no one I can go track down and take out, and there never will be because we already looked, didn't we? We tried to find out more about where he came from, but there was nothing but dead ends. Someone hurt our son, and there's not a damn thing I can do about it." He was seething with anger, his magic swirling around him in a wind of green with spots of blue. He was so pissed and upset he was shaking.

"Shh, A. It's okay."

"It's not fucking okay, Sebastian!"

"You're right, it's not okay. Whatever happened to Remi, it's not okay. But you need to remember that he's here with us now, and no matter what may've happened to him in the past, we are going to shower him with so much love, he's going to be smothered in it. He has you and me now, sweetheart, and he has a billion siblings that would go to war for him. He's loved, Ailin. He's loved and cared for, and no matter what happened before he came to us, we and our family are going to spend every day showing him just how much he's loved."

Ailin took a deep breath, and I could see him trying to ease his tension, and after two more deep breaths, he stepped up to me and leaned his forehead against my chest. I pulled him closer until he was flat against me, and he tucked his face into my neck. A shuddered breath left his lungs, and he finally started melting into me. His tension didn't disappear entirely, but I could tell he was a little calmer now as I held him and rubbed his back.

"I want to find whoever hurt him and make them suffer," he whispered, his voice sounding watery.

"I know, A, I know… I do too."

He nodded against me. "We almost lost him before we even knew him."

That made my heart hurt.

"If he wasn't a shifter, Seb… fuck! I can't even think—"

"Shh. I know, sweetheart. It's okay, he's okay." I held Ailin close. Even though Remi was here with us now, thinking about losing him was bringing back all those horrible feelings of losing his children that Ailin had after the war. Jorah, Thayer, and Basil might've come back after three years, but all the pain and hurt of thinking they were gone, of not being able to get to them for *years*, it was all still there. Nothing could erase that. "I've got you, A. I always do."

He nodded against me again, clinging to me, but he let me walk him back to the bed. We climbed in, and I pulled him into my arms under the covers, and I simply held him like I had so many times before when we'd been mourning our boys.

"I'm not going to let anyone hurt him ever again," Ailin whispered after he'd calmed some.

"Me either."

"He's going to know so much love, he won't know what to do with it."

I smiled against Ailin's hair. "We'll smother him in love."

He nodded. "Every day for the rest of his very long life."

"Yes."

He fell silent for a minute, then, "I'm sorry."

"What the hell for?"

"For breaking down… again."

I sighed. "Ailin, you're allowed your feelings."

"Maybe, but you always have to hold me together."

"That's what I'm here for. I hold you together when you break, and you keep me together when I shatter. We're partners, A, that's what we do. No matter what happens, we help each other through it."

He sighed and nuzzled into my neck. "I love you, Sebastian."

"I love you, too, A."

He smiled against my skin, kissed it, and we both closed our eyes, basking in our love for each other and the love we had for our family. Sometimes we might fracture, but we both knew that no matter what happened, we'd always be there for one another.

CHAPTER EIGHT

AILIN

Seraphina and Zammerra had taken it upon themselves to help Remi when he was in his wolf form. Our two Bonded ran with him and taught him how to be a wolf. They also decided they were his official babysitters anytime he was in that form. We kept a shield around the yard since we didn't want him traipsing through the trees at now nine months old, but Zamm and Sera stayed with him the entire time while Seb and I watched on from the porch.

The girls liked chasing and playing with him, so nearly every day all three of the kids plus our Bonded were running around like little maniacs. It was kind of wonderful.

The older kids and all the other adults in our coven were surprised that Remi was a shifter, but every single coven member had come to talk to Remi while he was in that form and to tell him how cute he was. They all petted him and let him know in their own way that he was accepted as he was, and I couldn't have been prouder of our coven.

"Alec wants us to take on some cases again," Seb said as we watched the kids playing from our chairs on the porch.

I looked at him. "Is that what you want?"

He shrugged. "The past couple months have been really great not having to work, but I do miss it sometimes."

I nodded. "Maybe we could do a part time thing."

"Opal is still willing to watch the kids when we're working, right?"

With a chuckle, I faced him. "She asked me the other day when we were going to get the hell out of here so she could spend time with her nieces and nephew."

He laughed. "That sounds like her."

"I think she misses helping out with the younger kids. She was always really great at it. She has more patience than anyone else I know."

He snorted. "Definitely more patience than you."

"Hey. I'm fucking patient."

Seb's eyes widened as he said, "The fact that you really believe that is actually fucking scary."

"You're an asshat."

"I can't believe you think you're patient."

"I have the patience of a saint."

He stared at me for a beat, then burst out laughing. "Oh my god. Ailin… seriously?" He laughed for a good five minutes straight.

"You are such a dick," I muttered.

"And you are the least patient person I know."

I flipped him off.

Seb chuckled. "The Food Twins also asked me about babysitting."

My eyes widened. "They did? They've never wanted to fucking help out before. Those little shits. I couldn't even get them to babysit at all once they moved out of the big house."

He shrugged. "I dunno. Jorah also volunteered, so obviously, if we want to go back to work, it won't be a problem logistically speaking."

Reading between the lines, I asked, "But it will be emotionally?"

Seb shrugged again, looking a little helpless, and he said, "I don't know yet. We didn't have that option with the other kids; we had to work, and then we had to… go to war. It just was what it was, you know? But it's different now."

"Do you want to quit?"

His eyes widened. "What? No. No way."

I couldn't help but smirk. "You're not making any sense."

He sighed. "I know. Maybe we can try a simple case that won't take long and see how it goes."

"I'll tell Alec."

Seb glanced at me. "What about you? Do you want to go back?"

"Yeah, kinda. I want to work, but nothing like we were before. I want to be here as much as possible, but I think it might be good for me to be out sometimes."

"Okay. We'll try it."

A little while later, I said, "It's kind of hot out."

"Okay…?"

"Maybe you should take your shirt off."

Seb rolled his eyes at me. "You're the one that's hot, you take off your shirt."

"Oh, detective, you just want to check me out. Should you be doing that with the kids right there?"

"Idiot."

I smirked. "Seriously, take off your shirt."

"No."

"Please?"

"Fucking no, Ailin."

"Seb, come on."

"You'll have to wait until the kids are in bed, asshat." His cheeks burned pink—my favorite shade on him.

I grinned at him and said, "You're blushing."

"I am not." His cheeks flushed more.

"Yes, you are. After all these years, I can still make you blush."

"Ass."

I laughed and called on my magic to pull his chair closer to mine. He yelped in surprise when the wind dragged him over, then glared at me as I leaned over the chair's arm to kiss his cheek.

"Ugh." He pushed me a little, then must've changed his mind because he grabbed my collar and yanked me closer to plant a huge kiss on my lips.

With a chuckle, I grabbed the back of his head and pulled him in to deepen the kiss. Since we were outside with the kids, it didn't last nearly as long as I wanted it, but there was a promise of more from him, so I knew we'd have some fun tonight.

I stood and stretched, then held my hand out to Seb, saying, "Let's go show those little boogers how to play *Adha Teiche*." It meant *Wild Escape* in Caillea, but was just a silly outdoor game.

Seb smiled, took my outstretched hand, and let me pull him up. "I hardly know the rules to that one."

"I'll teach everyone."

He grinned at me. "That should be fun."

As we walked over to the kids and Bonded, I paused when we got close and saw what they were doing. They were all gathered in a circle, so I'd assumed they were watching Niya play in the dirt or something like that, but that wasn't it at all.

Leilani was sitting in the grass, and I could feel her pulling her natural nymph magic to create these translucent little butterflies. Seb stepped behind me to wrap his arms around my waist and rest his chin on my shoulder as we observed them.

There were butterflies of all different colors flying around the group, but Leilani was now only making pink ones. What I didn't think she realized was that her magic was so powerful that after the butterflies flew from her, instead of disappearing or evaporating, they were becoming more solid. She was creating real, live butterflies.

And she was doing it while giggling at Remi, who was yipping and running in circles and shaking, happy as can be in his wolf form. Leilani kept making the pink butterflies land on him.

Zammerra exchanged a look with Seb before the little dragon pulled on Niya's sleeve to get the four-year-old to chase her. The two of them took off, but Leilani was focused on Remi, so she didn't notice.

Seb and I stood there for a long time, content, happy to see our kids being sweet to each other. Finally, Leilani noticed us, and she immediately stopped.

"You don't have to stop," Seb said right away.

I added, "That's really fucking amazing, Lani. Don't stop on our account."

She bit her lip, then nodded and made a few more pink ones.

Seb asked, "Is your favorite color pink?" *It wasn't before they came home, that's why we painted her room blue.*

He was worried, so I patted his hand. *It's alright, baby.*

Leilani offered a tiny smile. "No, I still like blue, but Remi likes the pink ones best."

I felt Seb melt against my back. *She's making them for Remi. How sweet is that?*

I grinned and rested my head against his for a moment, then said to Leilani, "You know they're becoming living beings, right?"

She froze. "What?"

I pointed behind her where a dozen or so butterflies—live ones, not mist-like ones—were flying around. "It seems like they float around you, then pass through your aura a second time and become solid."

She stared at the butterflies open-mouthed. "What. The. Hell."

I couldn't contain my snort. "Pretty cool, kiddo."

"How am I... I mean, but... I'm only a half-nymph." She blinked wide eyes at me.

I shrugged. "I think we need to find someone to help train you. Your magic is different than mine. I can help with some basics, but you're clearly a strong nymph, so I won't be able to help with everything."

She nodded slowly, gaping at the butterflies again. "I just wanted to play with Remi... he likes when I make pink butterflies."

Seb released me and walked up to her, kneeling beside her. "This is a good thing, Lani. You have nothing to be afraid of."

"But..."

He sat down on the ground and stared at her for several minutes before sighing and saying, "Did you know that I grew up thinking I was human?"

Her brows furrowed. "No."

He nodded. "I thought I was a human until I was thirty-five years old and Ailin figured out how to break the cloaking spell that had been on me since I was a baby. Suddenly, I had all this power, this enchanter magic that no one knew how to control, and… it was scary. I was terrified, but you know what?"

"What?"

"Ailin helped me figure out how to use it, how to control my magic, and now I… I love my magic. I love being able to do things that I thought were impossible when I was only human. Now I can protect myself and my family with it, or I can just use it to flick a light on or off from across the room." That made her smile. "I guess what I'm trying to say is that it's okay to be scared or worried about the power you have, I get it, trust me. But you have Ailin, and you have me, and we will help you, Leilani. No matter what, no matter how strong your magic is, or even if it's not strong at all, none of that matters because we're here, and we will help you. I promise."

She nodded for a few seconds before she launched herself into Seb's arms. He was surprised for a moment, but easily caught her and hugged her tight.

Thank you for helping her, I said. He understood what she was feeling in a way I never would because I was born a witch and grew up in a magical household. The concept of not having power, or thinking that you didn't have much of it, was completely foreign to me.

Seb rolled his eyes at me over the top of Leilani's head and said through our link, *Don't be a dumbass. Don't thank me.*

With a smirk, I walked over to the pair and kissed the top of their heads, then bent down to scoop Remi up. He licked my face, making me chuckle, and I whispered, "Want to get a snack, then come back outside to play a new game?"

He yipped and nuzzled into my neck. I wasn't sure if he understood what I said, but he must've at least gotten the gist. He shifted back to his human form as I carried him, which made it a hard scramble to be sure I didn't drop him, but as soon as he was shifted, he hugged my neck. Remi was truly the sweetest little boy.

Leilani and Niya asked if they could walk around outside while we were visiting Jorah at his house on the lake. I was going to walk with them, but Leilani begged to go by themselves, and I made them promise a million times that they wouldn't walk into the woods where we couldn't see them and that under no circumstances were they allowed in the lake or even closer than five feet from its edge.

Jorah had invited us to his house to hang out since he knew we wanted a change of scenery. He'd been playing cards and other board games with the girls whenever he had off work, and he wasn't working today so we all thought it might be nice to spend time here with him. We were still on coven property, obviously, but it was nice to get out of the house with the kids for a bit.

Seb was in the kitchen with Jorah, who was holding Remi and sneaking him snacks, while my viramore threw some lunch together. I was peeking out the window every two seconds to make sure the girls were okay.

Jorah and Seb were laughing loudly, which made me turn to watch them for a few seconds. Jorah had been my youngest, my baby, before we adopted Leilani, Niya, and Remi, so sometimes when I looked at him, I could only see my baby. Other times, like now, I couldn't believe how old he was, that he was an adult. He was such a good kid, too, and made me so proud. Seeing him laugh and joke around with Seb and Remi made me so damn happy.

I opened my mouth to ask what was so funny when we heard a loud, terrified scream coming from outside. All three of us were on the move without a thought. We dashed outside, and Jorah somehow flung Remi into Seb's arms before he used his nature magic to fly himself forward toward Niya, who was soaking wet and screaming at the top of her lungs at the edge of the water.

Jorah got there first, and all Niya did was point at the lake and yell, "Leilani!" before Jorah dove into the water.

Seraphina shifted to her manticore form and began flying above the water, searching for Leilani, and Zammerra made herself bigger, diving into the water with Jorah.

The water dragonettes that lived in our lake were squealing and flipping out, diving in and out of the water, obviously trying to help. The water sprites were chittering away, flipping out and pointing from the shore, and the water nymph that lived in our lake—a full nymph that changed form from a sort of fae-looking creature to one that was all water—came rushing over in her water form.

I looked at the nymph that I'd saved long ago from another witch that had tried to enslave her and said, "You can't have her, Ethemea! Give me my daughter back!"

She looked shocked for a split-second before she dove into the water.

Jorah popped up in the water, took a breath, and dove back down, and I dove in after him with Ethemea right beside me and Seb's voice echoing *Oh my god, oh my god, oh my god,* right in my head.

CHAPTER NINE

SEBASTIAN

Niya's terrified screams filled me with dread. I held Remi close in my arms and ran up to Niya, pulling her into my side. She was sobbing and screaming for her sister and sounded so pained and terrified, and I didn't know what to do to help. Ailin disappeared under the water, so I said in a shaky voice, "It's going to be okay, Niya. They'll find her."

She sobbed and leaned into me. Ailin, Zamm, and Jorah all popped up again without Leilani, each took a breath, then dove back under, and Niya wailed as I tried to keep it together. But tears were pouring down my cheeks.

Niya pulled out of my arms and rushed forward to the edge of the water. I ran after her and grabbed her arm so she didn't try going in after her sister, but she shrugged me off with more force than I thought possible from a four-year-old.

She squatted down, shoved her hands into the lake water, and her aura came off of her so powerfully and suddenly that it made me stumble back a few steps. The water began to glow around Niya's hands, and the glowing brightened as it moved farther and farther away from her. When it reached the middle of the lake, another powerful force pushed me backward like a shockwave.

"Niya," I said as I regained my footing and moved to her, placing my hand on her shoulder. She didn't shrug me off this time, she leaned into me.

Ailin and Jorah came up and climbed onto the rock wall that went at least twenty feet into the water.

Waves began to form in the lake, from the center out as the glowing from Niya intensified. The waves slowly started to grow bigger and bigger, but when they reached the shore, they were splashing around us, not on top of us, and then I noticed that they weren't crashing on Ailin and Jorah either.

"Holy shit," I whispered.

Just keep holding onto her, Seb, Ailin said in my head. *Don't let her go, and if that water nymph comes over there, don't you dare let her touch our daughter.* His voice was shaking with fear and tears, the same I felt in me.

I'll protect her.

I know you will.

I stared with wide eyes as our little Niya made these powerful waves and used magic, strong as hell magic, that I didn't understand. I didn't let go of her shoulder; I would support her no matter what happened. *Please let this work, whatever she's doing, please let it work.*

The waves moved back and forth, and after what felt like an eternity, a wave lifted Leilani from the depths of the lake to the surface. I gasped when I saw how blue she was, and even from far away, I could tell that she wasn't breathing.

"No, no, no," I whispered, my heart in my throat, tears falling freely. "Lani."

Zammerra and Seraphina flew over, landing behind me before they curled around my legs, once again in their small forms.

Ailin and Jorah rushed back to shore as the wave gently pulled Leilani over to Niya, placing Leilani right in front of her on the sand. Niya gasped and released all of her magic, then immediately collapsed, but I managed to keep her from hitting her head on the ground. I pulled her into my chest, Remi in one arm, Niya in the other, just as Ailin skidded to a stop beside Leilani. Niya wasn't passed out, but she had used so much magic that she was weakened, and she was crying as she stared at her unconscious sister.

"She's not breathing," he said as he gathered his green nature magic around him. He placed one hand on her forehead and the other on her chest and pushed with his magic as Sera jumped to his shoulder and curled around his neck.

He was trying to push the water out of Leilani's lungs.

Since we were linked by our viramore connection, I pushed my magic into him and into his spell. My enchanter magic could be more compatible with Leilani's nymph magic than Ailin's was since they both originated in Faela. And on top of my enchanter magic, I would always have a little bit of dragon magic inside of me from Zammerra's mother.

My purple dragon magic would always do surprising and amazing things because dragons were such magical creatures. It had saved my life, saved my soul, a long time ago, so maybe it would do the same for Leilani.

Ailin didn't acknowledge my blue and purple magics being added to his green, but I knew he appreciated it. He was one of the best healers I knew, but my magic could give him a boost.

Green, blue, and purple swirled around Leilani and Ailin, and I watched with my heart in my throat as the purple dragon magic concentrated on Leilani's chest, right over her heart.

"Come on, Lani," Jorah whispered before grabbing one of Lani's hands in both of his and pushing his nature magic and his Power of Three magic into her. His Three magic also originated in Faela, so hopefully it would be helpful here.

When nothing happened, a small sob came out of Ailin's chest, and I almost crumbled to the ground. He was beginning to panic because she wasn't responding. His fear and anguish were adding to my own. The only thing keeping me upright was the fact that I was holding Remi and Niya.

Even though I could feel Ailin's panic, he wasn't giving up, he pushed his magic harder, using more power and forcing the healing magic into her body.

But nothing happened.

"Ailin," I whispered after a few minutes. "Ailin." My voice cracked.

"No. No, I don't accept this. She can't be... she has to..." He broke off and sobbed, giving his magic another push.

Nothing happened.

I cried, my body trembling as I whispered, "Ailin."

His agonized eyes met mine and he whispered, "Seb, I can't... she's not..."

"A... it's okay."

He shook his head. "I can't do this... I can't..." *I can't lose another child.*

"I know, sweetheart." I buried my face against Remi as a loud sob came out of me, and I felt Ailin's magic easing off of our little girl.

Niya whispered, "Daddy? Why isn't she waking up?"

Ailin's sob sounded loud in the hushed silence of all the creatures from the lake surrounding us. *Daddy.* Oh god. My Bonded hopped up to curl around my neck.

"Seb," Ailin whispered. He needed me. I needed to hold him.

I started to get up, and Remi wiggled in my arms, suddenly shifting into his wolf form. He wiggled so crazily that he leapt out of my arms. Since I only had one arm to try to catch him with—the other holding Niya—he got away. "Remi!" I yelled, afraid that he'd go into the water, but thank god he only walked over to Leilani.

Our little wolf shifter climbed onto Leilani's chest and began licking her face, and the sight made me cry. He wanted his sister to wake up, but she wouldn't... she couldn't. I pulled Niya into my lap as I fell to my knees, and Ailin met my eyes, his were red-rimmed and overflowing.

"Dad?" Jorah said. "Try again."

"What?" Ailin turned to Jorah.

Jorah grabbed Ailin's hands and placed them back on Leilani's body. "Keep pushing."

"Jor..."

"No, just... just try." Jorah was crying, too. "Please, I have this... in my gut... you need to try again."

"Okay." Ailin always listened to his gut and trusted his instincts, and taught all his kids to do the same, so if Jorah felt something, he'd listen. If there was a tiny shred of hope, we'd take it.

Both Jorah and Ailin pushed their magic into Leilani again as Remi continued to lick her face. The green, blue, and purple swirled around the group, and after a few seconds, another color was added in. A pale pink magic that I'd never seen before. It was coming from Remi, his shifter magic.

Remi whined on Leilani's chest and stood up to lick her eyes as his pink magic grew stronger. Ailin and Jorah started chanting a healing spell, and I pushed my magic into it, reaching out to grab Leilani's ankle. Niya placed her hand beside mine on Leilani's leg. Our magics grew and darkened, thickened, swirling around us in an almost viscous manner. Jorah's Three magic sparked, like lightning bolts striking around us.

The magical cloud grew huge, tall up into the sky, and everything began to brighten. It started with a light glow that rapidly grew brighter until it was so bright, we had to shut our eyes to block it. The magical cloud exploded out in a huge shockwave of magic that made the trees rustle and the water ripple and wave.

And then the most beautiful sound I'd ever heard filled my ears.

A breath.

One sweet, tiny little breath.

A choked sob came out of me as Ailin let out a watery laugh and bent down to rest his forehead against Leilani's, and he pushed more healing magic into her. She began coughing, so Jorah pulled Remi off her, and Ailin helped Leilani sit up and turn to the side to throw up all the water she'd swallowed.

He rubbed her back, and I grabbed her hand as I scooted closer to her. Ailin was running his hands over her head, face, and arms, checking for other injuries and whispering, "I've got you, you're okay. Just get it out. You gotta get the water out of your system. You're okay, munchkin. You're okay." He was still crying, so was I. "I love you. You're going to be okay."

As soon as she finished puking her guts out, Niya launched herself into her big sister's arms, and Leilani coughed again, but hugged her.

Niya started talking a million miles per hour. "I'm sorry. I shoulda listened, Lani. I'm sorry, sorry. Sorry. I'm so sorry. I promise I'll listen. I shoulda listened. I'm sorry."

"It's okay," Leilani whispered, her voice hoarse and cracking.

Jorah kissed Leilani's hair as he stood and said, "I'll go get her some water." Remi yipped in my direction, so I took him from Jorah before Jor ran to his house.

Ailin pulled both girls into his arms. "You scared the shit out of me." I moved closer to join in until all five of us—plus Zamm and Sera —were in a big hugging pile.

Jorah came back over and paused, but Ailin and I both held an arm out until he came and joined our hug.

When Remi started barking out a complaint, we all released each other, Jorah gave Leilani the water he'd brought, and Ailin said, "You need to tell me what happened."

Niya opened her mouth, but Leilani said, "Niya jumped in even though I told her not to, and she went too deep, so I went in after her. I grabbed her and started walking back, but I slipped and… I think I hit my head on a rock or something. I don't really remember what happened after that."

Niya's lip quivered as she began crying again and mumbling, "I'm sorry," over and over.

Ailin, more calmly than I'd expected, said, "You can't go out into the water without an adult with you, Niya. I told you this a million times. You can't go into the lake or a pool or anywhere in the water without permission from me or Papa."

"Okay," she whispered. Her big bright blue eyes filled with tears. "Are you sending us back now?"

Ailin jerked back as if she'd slapped him, then his eyes widened and he said, "No. You're never going back there again, Niya. You are my daughter, and nothing you do will ever fucking change that. You are mine, Niya Bridgid Ellwood. You are my daughter. Period."

She swallowed hard, her little lip still quivering. "Promise?"

Knowing what Ailin needed, I pulled Leilani into my chest so she could lean on me, and Ailin grabbed Niya, pulling her into his arms and hugging her tight. "I promise, pumpkin. You never have to worry about that, never. You're stuck with me."

"And with me," I added. "You're mine as well, Niya."

Jorah cleared his throat and said, "And you're my sister, both of you are." He scratched the top of Remi's head. "And you're my little brother."

Remi yipped at him and tried to jump out of my arms, so Jorah grinned and picked him up for me, receiving a million wolf pup kisses.

I hugged Leilani and kissed her forehead. "You are mine as well, Lani. You're my daughter, and I swear if you ever scare me again the way you did today, I will lock you in your bedroom so you can never get hurt again."

She laughed a little, then wrapped her arms around my waist and tucked her head against my chest. "I'll try not to scare you again, Papa."

My eyes filled with tears hearing her say that for the first time, and I squeezed her, dropping a kiss to her head. "I love you, Lani."

"I love you, too." Her voice was quiet and hesitant, but heartfelt.

I held her tight, squeezed my eyes closed, and thanked every god and higher being out there for bringing our little girl back to us.

After several minutes, Ailin and I switched kids, by some unspoken rule or something. All four of us moved until I had Niya in my lap and Ailin was hugging Leilani tight.

I heard Ailin whisper, "I love you, kiddo."

And Leilani whispered back, "Love you too, Dad."

I smiled at them and hugged Niya to me, whispering, "You know I love you, right, my little pumpkin pie?"

"I know," she whispered, then yawned and added, "Love ya," before burying her head in my chest and falling asleep.

Ailin caught my eye over Leilani's head and said, "We should get them home. They need to be cleaned up, and Niya obviously used too much of her aura magic. We should ask Talon to come check her."

Jorah said, "I'll call Talon to meet us at the big house." He stood up, cradling a naked baby in his arms. "Um… his clothes are shredded."

"We better hurry before he pees all over you then," Ailin said to him.

Jorah rolled his eyes, checked that Niya and Leilani weren't looking at him, then flipped Ailin off, making us chuckle. After everything that just happened, I was surprised we were even able to smile, let alone laugh. Jorah hurriedly walked to the path that led to the big house, obviously wanting to get the baby wrapped up.

I held Niya in my arms, and Ailin helped Leilani stand up. When she wobbled, he asked, "Can I carry you?"

She didn't seem thrilled with the offer, but sighed and nodded, so he scooped her up.

The water nymph Ethemea came over, and Ailin stopped walking and threw up a shield in front of the four of us before I could even blink.

Ethemea froze, staring at him in shock. "Sage?" she whispered in Fae'lee—the language of the fae.

Through our link, I asked, *What are you doing? She's not dangerous.*

Normally, no, but she might think she has the right to take Niya.

What? Why the fuck would she think that?

Because Niya clearly has a strong water affinity, and she's a fucking water nymph. They keep their own.

I wasn't exactly sure what that meant, but I didn't like the sound of it.

Out loud, Ailin said, "You can't have her."

Ethemea put her hand over her heart, and I tried not to look at her bare breasts. Being a nymph, she didn't tend to wear clothes very often—or at all. She lived in and around the water, keeping to herself and wanting nothing to do with humanity after she'd been captured by a cruel man before Ailin saved her and offered her sanctuary. She very much was a nymph in the sense that she had connected to this lake and felt like it was hers, hers to guard, hers to care for.

She quietly said in her musical voice in Fae'lee, "I wanted to apologize to you, Sage. I was not in the water when the little nature nymph fell under. I'm sorry my lake took her, but I'm glad the water youngling was able to pull her sister out. I wanted to offer... my services if either of the halflings need help."

"You can't have them, Ethemea," Ailin repeated in Fae'lee. "They are my and Sebastian's daughters. You can't have them."

"I understand, Sage. I would never take them from you."

At that, Ailin relaxed and dropped his shield. Fae were many things, but liars they were not. Ailin said, "Thank you for the offer, Ethemea. If we need help, I'll seek you out."

She gave him a nod, then smiled softly at Leilani, then at Niya—who was still asleep in my arms—and then she nodded at me before transforming into water that was shaped like a person. She walked to the edge of the lake and sort of melted into it. The first time I'd seen her do that, it freaked me out, but at this point, I'd seen so much crazy and fucking weird shit that it hardly registered as odd.

But Leilani gasped and blinked at the water, then shook her head and rested it on Ailin's shoulder. The two of us began the trek back to the big house.

When we got there, Talon and Jorah were in the living room, sitting on the loveseat. Jorah was dry and clean and was holding a now-dressed Remi in his lap. Ailin and I walked into the living room, and Ailin used his magic to clean the four of us up. Niya still slept, so I kept her in my lap but sat on the couch, and Ailin carried Leilani over as Zammerra climbed off my shoulder to curl up on Niya's lap. Ailin set Lani down beside me—Seraphina crawled onto her lap and began purring as she petted her—then my viramore took the seat on the other side of her so we were all close.

Talon came over, placed his hand on Niya's forehead, and closed his eyes for a few minutes. When he opened them, he smiled at me. "She didn't do any permanent damage. She simply used a lot of her magic, but she didn't harm herself. She'll likely be tired for the rest of the day, perhaps tomorrow as well, and she may need more to eat."

"But she's okay?" I asked to clarify.

"Yes. She's perfectly fine. Having her father hold her"—he nodded at the way I was cradling her like a baby—"will help her aura heal more efficiently."

"It will?"

He nodded. "Family ties and affection always help."

"Oh."

Talon smiled. "Yes, Seb, it still works even though you're not blood related. All that matters is the connection, the family love. And of that, I'm sure there is plenty."

"Oh," I said again, then added, "Thank you."

He nodded with a grin, then moved over to Leilani. He checked her over and said, "Your aura is strong, Leilani."

"Thanks," she said, her cheeks turning pink. I was happy to see her getting some color back.

"Thank you for coming, Talon," Ailin said. "Will you stay for dinner?"

Talon smiled at him and exchanged a look with Jorah before saying, "Of course. Thank you, Sage."

Ailin groaned. "Don't you dare start calling me that. You're family, you don't call me by my title." *I hate that fucking title,* I heard him think, not purposefully including me in that thought but thinking it loudly enough that I overheard.

I smirked at him, and he rolled his eyes.

Talon chuckled.

Ailin narrowed his eyes at him. "You did that on purpose."

Talon put a hand to his chest, faking shock. "I would never."

Ailin chuckled and shook his head. "Alright, I think tonight calls for some pizza. I'll order a whole bunch and someone can run down to pick it up at the border of our wards. What does everyone want?"

As if sensing there was a food discussion happening, Niya opened her eyes and yelled, "Pineapple!"

"Eww, gross, Ni," Leilani said. "Can I have extra cheese please?"

"You can have whatever you want," Ailin said, pulling her into his side and scooting close enough that his arm and her shoulder were pressed against my biceps.

As Niya and Leilani started arguing over what kind of pizza was the best pizza, Jorah sent a group text out to the entire family.

JORAH: EVERYONE IS FINE NOW, BUT THERE WAS AN ACCIDENT AT THE LAKE with the girls. They're FINE. We're having pizza night at the big house, so come over. And give Lani, Ni, and Remi extra hugs.

SOMETIMES THAT KID WAS TOO SWEET FOR HIS OWN GOOD.

Before we knew it, the entire house was filled with our family checking on the little kids, and Ailin was putting together the biggest pizza order I'd ever seen.

While the girls were distracted by Basil and Thayer making them giggle, I asked Ailin through our link, *How is Niya a water nymph? Leilani is a nature nymph, just like their mother. I didn't think they could... cross over like that.*

I'm guessing that one of their grandparents was a water nymph and it runs in their family. You're right, though, normally a nature nymph can only have a nature nymph, but it's possible to have different types if there's a close blood relative, like a parent or grandparent.

I was quiet for a minute, then said, *I wonder if it's in their files. It has their lineage, at least what's known of their ancestry. I know none of their family survived the war, but I'm curious.*

We'll check, and if it's not there, we can get the information. It'd be nice to have it on hand in case the girls want to know anything about their biological family when they're older.

I reached over and grabbed his hand so I'd have some kind of contact with him. *That's a good idea. I wish we had that for Remi, too.*

So do I.

I kissed his knuckles, then refocused on our family.

At one point, Emrys came over, sat on the coffee table in front of Ailin, and after giving the girls each a hug, said, "This is really terrible timing, but can you come in this week?"

Ailin groaned. "Seriously, Em?"

"They're talking about taking away some of the funding for the displaced kids again, and nothing I say is swaying the vote," Emrys said.

Ailin pinched the bridge of his nose with his free hand and sighed. "Why wouldn't they listen to you?"

He made an impatient and annoyed sound in the back of his throat as he sat up. "We need the witch representatives to vote on keeping the funding."

"But you're one of the witches on the board, why can't you work your charm on them?"

"All they see when they look at me is a vampire, and..." Emrys turned his head to offer his viramore Julius a small smile before coming back to this conversation. "Unfortunately, most people don't think vampires have the kids' best interests in mind."

Ailin grunted. "That's fucking bullshit. They've known you for years, they know how hard you fought for people's rights even before the war, they know you're both witch and vampire, why the hell wouldn't your opinion matter now?"

Emrys shrugged. "Sometimes the prejudices are too strong. The world is a hell of a lot better and getting better every day, but those things don't just disappear overnight. Please help me."

"You know I will," Ailin said, dropping a kiss to Leilani's hair. "Tell me when and where, and while we're at it, let's get Petunia to set up a fundraiser for Eastbrook and all the programs that are helping displaced kids and young adults. We need that funding, but even that isn't enough."

Emrys smiled, stood, and patted Ailin's shoulder. "Thank you, Lin."

Ailin nodded at him, then turned to me with a grimace. "Looks like you're going to have them by yourself again."

"It'll be fine." I rolled my eyes.

Leilani said, "I'll help this time, Papa."

My heart swelled so big, I couldn't speak.

Ailin shot her an appreciative smile and hugged her tight, resting his head on hers. "That would be great, Lani."

Remi was passed from coven member to coven member, and the

little squirt was eating up all the attention. Leilani and Niya were both too worn out, so the four of us and our two Bonded stayed huddled together for the rest of the night with the rest of the family coming by to check on the girls.

As I'd done many times over the years, I sat back and smiled. This crazy, beautiful, wonderful family was filled with more love than I ever thought possible, and I was beyond grateful that they'd not only welcomed me in with open arms, but now they were happy and excited to have our family grow. They supported me in everything, including adopting three new kids with Ailin, and now these crazy, amazing people were showering Leilani, Niya, and Remi with their love. And it was a beautiful thing to watch, and even better to be included in it.

CHAPTER TEN

AILIN

The Brinnswick Union meeting I'd attended with Emrys and Julius six months ago had been one annoyance after another. Even though some of the asshole officials pissed me off with wanting to allocate the displaced children's fund for other things, I understood where they were coming from because they wanted to use it for other good programs. Like putting more money into the rebuilding projects and helping small businesses that suffered during the war and needed a boost to get restarted. So at least these people weren't actual assholes, they were simply trying to help in other areas.

Still, they couldn't take money away from the kids. Eastbrook was *finally* doing an amazing job with the children that had already suffered through tragedy; we couldn't make them suffer again.

It was a pain in the ass, but Emrys, Julius, and I won the vote to keep the money going to the kids. But I'd also promised to help set up some fundraisers and other shit for the other programs. Which apparently had become a thing I did since right now, we were on our way to the annual Eastbrook Youth Academy fundraiser that Seb and I helped set up.

"How did I become in charge of fundraising? What the fuck are these people thinking?" I asked Seb, who was driving. The kids had been with us for over nine months now, so he was comfortable behind the wheel.

He chuckled. "They're thinking that you have a million contacts that you're not afraid to talk into helping out. They're thinking that you've helped with Eastbrook, so you know what you're doing."

"But I don't. I helped, I didn't fucking run the damn thing." I sighed and put my foot up on the dash. Seraphina rubbed her cheek against mine since she was curled around my neck. I was surprised she hadn't hopped over to Seb yet; she usually did when we were in the car. Or standing outside. Or in the house. Or anywhere, really.

Sera made an annoyed sound at me, then licked my cheek and nuzzled into me. "I know you love me. I love you too, Sera."

Seb rubbed my thigh. "You'll do fine."

I grumbled and turned to stare out the window.

Seb glanced in the rearview mirror before focusing on the road once more. "Leilani, you didn't have any homework this weekend, did you?"

"No, Papa, she doesn't usually give us homework on the weekends," she answered as she petted Zammerra, who was contentedly curled up in her lap.

"Okay, just checking." He nodded. "Ni, what do you have in your hands?"

Niya sighed. "It's Scout from school."

Seb and I groaned together, and I turned in my seat to shoot our daughter a glare. "Ni, we told you to leave him at home for this so he doesn't get lost. You have to leave him in the car, okay?"

She pouted, her cute bottom lip sticking out, her eyes big and round with the cutest and saddest little expression on her face. She got away with so much when she made that face, and she knew it, too. "But it's my turn to keep him."

Before I could give in and tell her she could bring the stupid preschool classroom stuffed animal puppy with her, Seb pushed my face back with his large hand.

"Hey!" I yelled, scooting back.

"Don't look at her when she's making that face," he said, making

Leilani crack up. Through our link, he added, *I know you'll give her anything she wants.*

Because it's the cutest thing I've ever seen. How can something so sweet be such a terror?

His groan turned into a chuckle. "I have no idea."

I shot him a grin, then kept facing forward as I said, "No, Niya, Scout stays in the car."

She grunted in frustration, and I could practically feel her glare on the back of my head, but I refused to look.

"Stay strong," Seb said, making me and Leilani chuckle.

When we pulled up to the carnival outside of the Eastbrook Youth Academy, Seb found a parking spot, but it took a long time. Which meant there were a lot of people here, and that was exactly what we needed.

Once we parked, I grabbed the stroller from the trunk and Seb and the girls got out. I saw Seb take Scout out of Niya's hands and place him back into the car, leaving Niya pouting. Leilani nudged Seb with her shoulder and smiled up at him with Zammerra curled around her shoulders. He grinned at her and took Niya's hand in his.

I unhooked Remi from his car seat, and he yelled, "Dada!" at me.

I rubbed our noses together as I buckled him into the stroller, and he giggled. "No shifting while we're here, okay? I don't want you to get hurt."

He grabbed my cheeks and smooshed them together, so I took that as agreement. There were bound to be all types of people here, including humans, so I didn't want Remi to shift and have people freak out, and for Remi—or someone else—to get hurt in the panic. He was honestly really good about knowing the time and place to shift.

At least, he had been since he shifted on me in the middle of the grocery store about a month ago. The humans in the aisle had freaked out and started yelling "Werewolf!" and pointing at the tiny pup in my cart that was wagging his tail at them. They acted like he was a feral animal about to attack. They'd caused a store-wide panic, and BCA agents showed up. It had been traumatizing for my little man—and for me, especially since I hadn't been allowed to just blast the bastards away—and the entire family had to spend the whole week trying to convince Remi that there was nothing wrong with his wolf form. Trying to make a fourteen-month-old understand that people were just assholes was not an easy feat. But as far as I could tell, he'd forgotten about the incident. One could only hope.

I kissed his nose and stood up, shoved the five trillion things we just *had* to fucking bring with us in the bottom basket, then pushed the stroller over to Seb and the girls. The older kids were all meeting us here later on, coming in their own vehicles since they were coming from different places. We were all supposed to go on the merry go round together once everyone arrived. It was probably the only ride everyone was allowed on, including Remi, and when Opal had suggested it, nearly everyone thought it was a fun idea.

"Lead the way, Papa," I said to Seb.

He nodded at me and asked, "Where to first, girls? Wanna go on a few rides, then get some cotton candy and play a few games?"

"Yes!" Niya squealed at her normal Niya volume—also known as loud as shit.

Leilani shrugged. "Whatever." She was trying to be all cool-pre-teen, but I could see her excitement.

"Remember the rules," Seb said. "You have to stay together and stay within my and Daddy's sights at all times."

"I know, Papa!" Niya said. "Promise!"

"If you break the rules, we will leave."

"I *know*," she said.

We spent the next hour following them around and watching their excited faces on rides. Seb took Remi on a little train ride that went less than a mile an hour in a small circle, but Remi was so excited and cute that I took him on the next one. Seb took pictures of the kids on every single thing they rode.

There was a crazy twirling ride that went fast enough your body stuck to the walls or something while it tilted and moved all over the place, and of course, our crazy child wanted to ride it. I was secretly happy when she wasn't tall enough to go, but I felt bad afterward, so...

we were now the proud owners of a goldfish. A goldfish that was absolutely miserable inside a little bag. *I wonder how much trouble I'd get in if I set all those bagged fish free? Those poor things.*

"Don't even think about it, A."

"Think about what?"

Seb rolled his eyes. "We're not sneaking back in here after it closes to steal all those fish."

I said, "I wasn't thinking that."

"Uh huh. As if I can't read your mind. Where the hell would you even put them?"

"I could build a pond in the yard."

"Ailin, they're fine. They'll go to good homes soon."

I frowned at him. "They're not fine."

He sighed. "You can't save a thousand goldfish, A. Just leave it."

I stared at the little fish.

"Sweetheart, there's nothing you can do now, but if it upsets you that much, you can request that they don't have that game here next year."

"Of course it upsets me. You know I want animals to be free."

"I know." *But our daughter is excited about having a pet, even if it's just a goldfish that'll only live for a few months.*

You cheater. You played the daughter card.

He snorted. "Yep, and I'll do it again if I have to."

I sighed. Now we were going to have to make a pitstop at a pet store because I didn't know if I could put the little guy in the lake.

Seb shook his head at me with a grin. "You're going to buy the most extravagant tank for that goldfish, aren't you?"

I lifted a shoulder. "Obviously. He deserves a good home. Look at his little face."

He chuckled and asked Niya, "What do you want to name your fish?"

She tilted her head, examining him as I held the bag up, and then she smiled really wide and yelled, "Armpit!"

A bark of laughter came out of me before I could help it, Seb tried to hide his laugh but failed, and Leilani yelled, "Ew, Niya, we're not naming our fish Armpit! Who in the bloody hell names a fish *Armpit?*" Well, she was obviously fitting in with the Ellwoods quite well now.

"You said a bad wo-ord," Niya sing-songed—she loved teasing her sister with that—then she shrugged and said, "He looks like an armpit."

I couldn't help my chuckle.

"I refuse to call him that." Leilani crossed her arms over her chest.

Niya pursed her lips. "Fine. What about Booger?"

"No," Lani said.

"Nose?"

"What? No."

"Weiwani?"

"Seriously, Niya? No. Mother of All."

"Poopy Head?"

"No!"

"Mr. Wiggles?"

"N—wait, uh… sure. I guess."

I laughed. "Alright, everyone, meet Mr. Wiggles."

Leilani sighed, Remi said something that sounded like "Wiggy," and Seb chuckled before moving us along.

When the rest of the family met us, I was already exhausted and ready to go home, but then everyone decided they were hungry, so we got some—very expensive—carnival food that was pretty damn delicious. Kinda made the whole thing worth it.

Mrs. Hunley found us as she made rounds, and she came over to give me a hug, then fussed over the girls and Remi for a few minutes. When she came to stand beside me, she said, "Thank you for helping get us some good deals and so many donations for the silent auction."

I waved her away. "No big deal."

Watery eyes met mine as she grabbed my wrist. "It is a big deal, Ailin. You've been such a huge help and a wonderful advocate for us, and there's nothing I could do to show you just how much I appreciate it, but thank you. For everything."

I didn't know what to say to that, so I gave her a single nod, and when she chuckled at me, I accepted the hug she offered.

The rest of the evening turned into me following my kids—of all ages—all around the whole damn carnival until I felt like my feet were going to fall off. Luckily, our stroller had one of those extra seats for bigger kids, so Niya was able to take breaks as she needed them. Unfortunately for Seb and me, it meant pushing extra weight.

By the time we got home and fell into bed together, I honestly didn't think I could move an inch. I fell onto my stomach, and after a minute, I decided that was exactly where I'd stay until morning, even if I really did wish I was under the blanket and that my boots were off.

Seb chuckled at me. "You're not sleeping like that."

"Not moving."

"Can you even breathe with your face in the mattress like that?"

"Eh. Breathing's overrated."

He snorted and walked over to my side of the bed and pulled me farther up, turning me on my side. When he tried to pull the blanket out from under me, he gave me a look until I finally moved enough that he could grab it. Then he took my boots and leg bracers off, and by the time he got to my arm bracers, I discovered that at least one part of my body wasn't ready for sleep yet.

Just as I was about to suggest he get naked, I heard a quiet, "Papa?"

I sighed, Seb smirked at me, obviously having known where my thoughts were going, then he pressed a quick kiss to my mouth and walked out of the room to Niya's.

I hadn't even realized I'd fallen asleep until I startled awake when Seb crawled back into bed. Rubbing my eyes and yawning, I asked, "Is she okay?"

"Yeah. Upset tummy, probably from the mountain of cotton candy she ate. I healed her as much as possible and gave her some water, made her go to the bathroom, and she went back to sleep. I won't be surprised if she crawls into our bed in a few hours, though."

I nodded and scooted over to lie on Seb's chest. He wrapped me in his arms and kissed my forehead, saying, "Today was fun."

"It was."

"But I'm glad it's only a once a year kind of thing."

I chuckled. "Me too, baby."

"Tomorrow's going to be a lazy day."

"Oh yeah. Maybe we can watch movies all day or something."

"That sounds perfect."

After a minute, I asked, "Do you miss going out and taking down bad guys?"

He snorted. "What do you mean? We're still doing stuff for the BCA."

"Yeah, but when we got together we were fighting… really evil shit."

"Yeah, and both of us almost died in the process… multiple times. Yeah, no thank you. I'm perfectly happy with doing easy jobs and getting to come home to our family every night. I love living a more peaceful life with you, Ailin."

I sighed and put my hand over his vitmea mark, claiming him like I always did.

A minute passed before he asked in a quiet and hesitant voice, "What about you, A? Do you miss it?"

"Hell no. Keeping you and the kids safe was all I ever wanted to do. I like doing all the little shit we get to do now that there's more peace in the world."

"I thought you liked going on adventures and stuff."

"I do, but the things we've been doing for work have more than filled that need." I kissed his cheek. "And anyway, raising these kids with you is turning out to be an adventure in and of itself."

He chuckled. "That's very true."

"Niya is a wild thing, and Remi seems like he's going to be a hand-ful, too."

"They're crazy." He hesitated, then sighed and said, "Lani told me earlier that there's a kid in her class that keeps picking on her."

I sat up to stare him in the eyes. "What?"

"Shit. I knew I shouldn't have told you."

"Sebastian Cooper Ellwood, tell me what the fuck you're talking about right now."

He glared at me. "First of all, don't talk to me like that, second of all, calm the hell down. Your magic is flying across the room."

I glanced around at the green wind flying around us and sighed, then closed my eyes and took a calming breath. When I had my magic under control, I stared him in the eye again. "Tell me what you're talking about."

He gave me the stink-eye, but said, "This boy's been picking on her for being half human."

"What the fuck?"

He sent me a sad smile. "Yeah, it's fucked up, but you know what she told him?"

"What?"

"That at least her family chose her instead of getting stuck with a jerk like him."

"Oh wow."

He nodded. "Yeah, she said that the kid is mean to everyone, and that she has it handled. If she needs our help, she promised she'll tell us."

"Okay." I calmed down even though I hated the situation.

Seb pulled my head back down to his chest. "The kid she's talking about is the one whose mom died in the war. His dad's a single parent, and I think they've been having a tough time, so he's obviously lashing out."

I nodded and sighed. "I guess that means we'll be seeing if we can help the little asshole?"

"As long as you don't call him a little asshole to his face, no matter how badly you want to. I want to tell him what a shit he's being, too, but… I'm not sure that's what he needs."

"Stop it with all your gross compassion, you're rubbing off on me."

He laughed. "I feel bad for the kid, I can't help it. I hate that he made Lani feel bad, but… he's obviously having a hard time."

I sighed. "We'll see what we can do."

He kissed my hair. "Good. But if that asshole keeps it up, we kick his ass."

"Sounds fair."

He rubbed my back and kissed my forehead. "Hey, A?"

"Hey, Seb?"

"I love you, and I love our life."

A smile tugged at my lips, and I leaned in to kiss his vitmea mark, then his chin, then his soft lips. He immediately deepened the kiss and pulled me on top of him. I groaned as I rocked my hips, and I thought to him, *I love you and our life, too, baby.*

A knock on the door made me groan in frustration, but the quiet, "Dads?" had me turning and calling back, "What's wrong?"

Leilani opened the door to our bedroom, wringing the bottom of her shirt and not looking us in the eye.

When she didn't say anything, I asked, "Did you have a nightmare, Lani?"

She nodded, and Seb and I exchanged a look. It wasn't the first time she'd had a nightmare, and it was shit but it likely wouldn't be her last. Usually they were about her biological parents dying, especially her mother since she remembered her mom covering her body in the explosion. I knew what it felt like to have your parents ripped from you, and I hated that she'd gone through that.

I moved back from Seb and lifted the blanket. "Come on up, Lani."

She rushed over and climbed over Sebastian to get in the middle of us, and the three of us settled down.

Seb asked, "Do you want to talk about it?"

Leilani shook her head. "No."

I opened my mouth, but Niya's voice said, "Daddy?"

I sighed and climbed out of bed, muttering, "They're never having cotton candy so close to bedtime ever again."

Seb chuckled and hugged Leilani while I went into Niya's room. As soon as I saw her, I lifted her out of bed and asked, "Want to sleep in my bed?"

She nodded.

"Okay, I'm going to check on your brother. Go on in with Papa, I'll be right there."

I kissed her cheek, put her down, and as she rushed across the hall, I padded over to Remi's room. I wasn't even surprised to see him sitting up in bed. Walking inside, I grabbed the little squirt out of his crib and carried him into our room.

Seb shook his head when he saw Remi in my arms, but he was smiling so I knew he didn't mind. Remi stayed beside me with Niya on his other side, then Leilani, and then Seb on the opposite side as me. When everyone was falling asleep, I reached over the pile of kids and took Seb's hand in mine, and finally, everyone began to fall into a peaceful sleep.

EPILOGUE

AILIN

FOUR YEARS LATER

I shoulder-bumped Seb, and he automatically put his arm over my shoulders to pull me against his side as he leaned against the house, watching the kids running around laughing. Well, Niya was running around with Remi trying to keep up with her, and Leilani was sitting on the porch drawing in her sketchbook and listening to music.

Seb and I stayed there in silence for a few minutes, both of us soaking up the comfort and joy of home and family, but after a while, I said, "They're pretty great, aren't they?"

"They are." He sighed and pulled me tighter to him. "We're lucky to have them."

I eyed my viramore for a moment and smirked. "You know what that means?"

He looked at me suspiciously. "What?"

"It's time to adopt more."

He stared at me for several beats before surprise registered on his face followed by horror. "Are you fucking kidding me, A?"

A chuckle came out before I could hold it in. "You love having kids."

"That doesn't mean I want more of them!"

"You know I'm going to convince you, so you may as well give in."

"Ailin, I swear to god if you're only saying this to get a rise out of me, I'm going to—"

"I'm not."

He snapped his mouth shut and stared at me for a long moment, then shut his eyes and muttered under his breath, "For fuck's sake."

"I think we need two more."

"No fucking way."

"Come on, baby, it'll be great."

"I think we have our hands full enough with these three and the *fifteen fucking others!*"

I shrugged. "None of them live with us anymore, though."

"Not the point."

"We're getting more, just you wait."

He sighed. "You're lucky I'm not strangling you right now."

I chuckled, stepped in front of him, and held onto his waist as I met his eyes. "You're gorgeous."

"Saying that isn't going to make me less pissed."

I laughed. "Trust me, I know."

He rolled his eyes at me and shook his head. "Ailin, are you being serious right now?"

"Yes."

"We're not going to fill every damn room in the house. That's not fucking happening, Ailin Talamh Ellwood."

"What if I promise that I'll stop asking for more after two more?"

"What if we simply wait for more grandkids instead?"

I groaned. "Don't say that."

He lifted a brow at me. "So you're okay with being a father to a thousand kids, but not a grandfather to one?"

"No, I love having a grandkid, but… I'm way too young to have a grandkid."

"So?"

I huffed and said, "You're frustrating."

"Not as frustrating as you."

"Why do you like arguing with me about everything?"

He just grinned at me.

"Whatever. I don't want the other kids getting any ideas and having kids yet. They're too young."

His grin grew.

"What, Sebastian?"

He chuckled. "You became their father when you were sixteen, and you think they're too young to have kids even though half of them aren't that much younger than you?"

"Yes."

He snorted. "You're ridiculous."

"They deserve to live their lives first. Having kids is a huge commitment, and they deserve to live and have fun for a while."

He stared at me for several seconds before nodding to himself. "So you want two more of your own?"

I smiled up at him. "Yes. I promise I'll stop asking after that."

"So twenty kids will finally be enough for you?"

"It's not twenty kids."

He said, "If you count Aspen, it is."

I opened my mouth, then snapped it shut when he started naming all the kids—in age order, too.

"Aspen, Opal, Pumpernickel, Pepper, Pear, Peach, Honey, Sugar, Willow, Basil, Thayer, Delaro, Clover, Tiordan, Jorah, Leilani, Niya, Remi. That's eighteen, Ailin. *Eighteen.*"

"That… sounds like a lot more when you list them like that."

He snorted.

"May as well make it an even twenty, right?"

He groaned and pinched the bridge of his nose, then released a sigh and pecked my lips. "I'll think about it."

I grinned from ear to ear. "That's a yes."

He shook his head and groaned again. "Why do I do this to myself?"

"Because you're a true softy."

He rolled his eyes and pointed over my shoulder. "You sure you want more? Our son is eating dirt right now." A look of horror crossed his face. "Oh god! He's trying to eat a worm!" I laughed as I released him to run across the yard while Seb yelled from the porch, "Don't do it, Remi! Oh god, ew. Don't eat that fucking disgusting thing!"

I made it to Remi just in time to grab his hand and whisper, "We don't eat bugs, buddy." Remi frowned up at me, so I leaned closer to him, lowering my voice further. "You know what we can do, though? We can chase Papa with it. He's scared of bugs."

Remi's answering smile was huge and made me chuckle as I scooped the little squirt off the ground, worm and all.

When I turned to head back toward Seb, he held his hands in front of him and said, "I swear to god, A, if you come over here with that thing, I'm going to blast your ass!"

Remi, the girls, and I all cracked up when I rushed closer and Seb screamed at the top of his lungs like he was being attacked by a fucking giant.

I had the best fucking family ever.

~

The End

Thank you so much for reading *The Enchanter's New Kids*. I hope you enjoyed getting to see a peek into Seb and Ailin's life after the war.

If you haven't read the spin-off series, *The Brinnswick Chronicles*, the first three books (*Thayer*, *Nikolai*, and *Basil*) are available now. The fourth book is Jorah's story and will be out in early 2021.

ABOUT MICHELE NOTARO

Michele is married to an awesome husband that puts up with her and all the characters in her head—and there are many. They live together in Baltimore, Maryland with their two young boys and two crazy dogs. She grew up dancing and swimming and taught dance—ballet, tap, jazz, hip hop, & modern—for ten years before her kids came along. Now she stays home to write about the sexy men in her head and does PTA everything—as long as coffee is involved. Two other tattooed moms run the PTA with her, and though she wants to rip her hair out from it, she still loves it.

MICHELE'S LINKS:
Website
Email
Facebook
Join my Newsletter to keep up to date on my upcoming books!
Facebook Reader Group: Notaro's Haven ~ stop by for exclusives, updates, and lots of fun!
If you're interested in more paranormal books and fun, check out the paranormal Facebook group, Reading Past the Realm, for more from me and many other authors!

Feel free to contact me on Facebook or email. I'd love to hear from you!

Dissolution

The Brotherhood of Ormarr: (Dragon Rider Romance)

Book 1: Azaran (by Jacki James)

Book 2: Zale (by Michelle Frost)

Book 3: Eeli (by Bobbie Rayne & Steph Marie)

Book 4: Malachite (by Michele Notaro & Sammi Cee)

Finding My Forever: (Contemporary Romance)

Everything In Between

A Little Bit Broken

Left Behind

A True Fit

A Finding My Forever Short Story: (Contemporary Romance)

Falling In Time

A Valentine's Tail

Flash Me Photos: (Contemporary Romance)

Love, Never-Ending

The Fate of Love Series: (Contemporary Romance)

Always You

My Forever: (Contemporary Romance)

Color My Kiss

Luck of the Ship

Interlocking Fragments: (Contemporary Romance Collab with Sammi Cee)

Heart Strain

Digging Deeper

Liberating Love

More to come in this series

Malachai Brothers: Behind the Veil: **(Paranormal- Ghosts- Collab with K.M. Neuhold)**

Akasha Sanatorium

Audiobooks:

The Enchanter's Flame

The Enchanter's Soul

The Witch's Blood

The Enchanter's Heart

How We Survive

Rescuing His Heart